Heart Of Stone

A John Smith short story

By Craig William Emms

Cold Fish Books

This novel is entirely a work of fiction.
The names, characters and incidents portrayed in it are
the work of the author's imagination or are used fictitiously

First published in Great Britain by
Cold Fish Books 2013

Copyright © Craig William Emms and Linda Barnett 2013

Craig William Emms asserts the moral right to
be identified as the author of this work

A catalogue record for this book is
available from the British Library

ISBN 978-0-9572168-5-3

All rights reserved. No part of this publication may be
reproduced, stored in a retrieval system, or transmitted,
in any form or by any means, electronic, mechanical,
photocopying, recording or otherwise, without the prior
permission of the Copyright owners

This book is dedicated to Barbara, Johnny and Angie.
Thanks for your help. You're the best of friends.

Also by Craig William Emms

ONE HEARTBEAT A MINUTE

PUBLIC ENEMY

THE STORY SO FAR...

Heart of Stone is the third story in the John Smith series, following on from *One Heartbeat a Minute* and *Public Enemy*.

In *One Heartbeat a Minute* we meet John Smith. He is an ex-Rhodesian and British Army Special Forces veteran who has fought in several brutal and bloody wars around the world including Afghanistan, the Falklands and the Gulf War. Smith has taken on guerrillas in Africa, terrorists in Northern Ireland and Libyan insurgents in Chad. He is a true warrior of the modern age... but has never been acknowledged as a hero...his work has been clandestine and "off the books". When he finally leaves the army, he is a broken and embittered man on the edge of insanity.

However MI6 refuses to leave Smith alone and his skills are put to use as an assassin, murdering enemies of the state in cold blood. Then, when he's of no more use to them, they frame him with the abduction, rape and murder of a little girl. They want to keep their dirty secrets to themselves and plan to have Smith locked away forever.

But John Smith is not the type of man to take such action lying down. He fights back, setting out on a rampage of death and destruction that shakes the establishment to its very core. Smith single-handedly takes on the system and leaves it in ruin. Then, with his sense of vengeance finally satiated, he flees from the UK to find himself something that he has never had before: a life of peace.

In *Public Enemy*, the second story in the series, John Smith faces his old nemesis, Alan Davies. Davies is the policeman who was in charge of investigating John as a suspected paedophile, but he is now working with MI6 to hunt John down and bring him to justice. This time though, MI6 are not prepared to see Smith go to prison for a crime he did not commit - they want his mouth shut forever. They want him dead.

Running for his life, Smith has to fight knife-wielding terrorists, an ex-IRA hit man employed by MI6 to kill him, Somali drug dealers and a bunch of vicious thugs who have kidnapped the Royal Couple. His skills and tenaciousness are tested to the limit in this non-stop all-action thriller with a twist in the tail.

Read on to find out what becomes of John Smith in *Heart of Stone...*

ONE

John Smith is dead, as far as the rest of the world is concerned, anyway. His body lies decomposing under millions of tons of rock in the Derbyshire Peak District after a suicidal mission to rescue the Duke and Duchess of Cambridge. His name will soon be forgotten too. You know what they say: Today's news is tomorrow's chip wrapper. Good riddance to bad rubbish. No one will miss him.

John Smith had been one of the best soldiers in the British Army, which meant literally that he had been one of the best soldiers in the world. He joined the army at the young age of sixteen as a boy soldier in the Parachute Regiment. After being locked up in the guardroom for being drunk and pissing on the Regimental Sergeant Major's car (not a thing that is easily forgiven – especially by the RSM), he was offered a *once in a lifetime* chance to earn brownie points from his country as an undercover operative in the Rhodesian Bush War. Being both youthful and stupid, he had jumped at the chance and given up his own identity and name for the first time, only to find that he could never go back to being who he had once been – ever. He was tasked with collecting intelligence about the war, and in particular attacks planned by the Rhodesian Special Forces against the leaders of the Zimbabwean guerrillas. The information that he gathered had been passed on to the guerrillas by the British government and had saved their lives on numerous occasions. As well as being a spy during this time, he had also served with distinction in some of the most famous Special Forces regiments, including the Selous Scouts and the Rhodesian Special Air Service Regiment.

After the Bush War he returned to the UK. Again he had changed his name, this time to John Smith, in order to prevent reprisals against him by some very pissed off Rhodesians who had once been his best friends. Back in the British Army, he was allowed to join the British SAS and had then enjoyed a full career of creating mayhem and mischief. He had served everywhere. From the gloomy streets of Belfast to the baking deserts of northern Chad and southern Libya, through to the sodden, rain-swept moors of the Falkland Islands. After being captured and horrifically tortured by the Soviets in the frozen mountains of Afghanistan, his career as a Special Forces soldier had eventually come to an abrupt halt. But his skills (perfected by many years of fighting in brutal conflicts and wars) had been needed by the Increment, a top secret arm of the British Secret Intelligence Service – MI6. By this time his mind had been battered to its core by his experiences turning him into an unthinking and cold-hearted killer, and so he had used his skills very effectively as an assassin for the British government, murdering and butchering his way through dozens of suspected and known terrorists. Finally, he had cracked completely under the strain and despite his long and distinguished career, he had been abandoned by the very Government that had used him so badly, and was thrown out on to the street. He had lost his career, his home and his family and had taken to the bottle in a big way.

Then had come the final insult: He had been framed as a murderer and paedophile by his former masters in an effort to keep him quiet about his work as an assassin. This would have worked wonderfully except that his former employers had forgotten one thing – John Smith was a hard, mean bastard who just would not lie down and take being framed. He escaped from the court where he was just about to be sentenced to life in prison and went on the rampage. He found the men who had framed him and killed them all, destroying as much of the police's infrastructure as he could on the way. Then he fled the country under yet another false name and identity, hoping against hope that he would never be found, and wishing nothing more than to end his years enjoying the two things that he had never had in his life – peace and quiet.

However, the Secret Intelligence Service was just as stubborn and unforgiving as John Smith. They tracked him down to his hiding place in the Gambia, West Africa, intent on silencing him for good this time. He escaped by the skin of his teeth only to find himself on an aircraft that was hijacked by fanatical Islamic terrorists. Once again he had to fight for his life. He won through but had been severely injured during the ensuing fight. His life was saved on the operating table only because of the skill of a female surgeon from Australia; a woman who he eventually fell in love with.

Badly wounded and tired to his very soul of fighting, Smith had been sent to prison for the crime that he had never committed. But you can't keep a good man down for ever and eventually he had conned his way on to a team concerned with rescuing the Duke and Duchess of Cambridge, who had been kidnapped and held hostage by a group of pissed-off former British soldiers who called themselves 'The Brotherhood'. The kidnapping was not as it appeared however as Smith and the kidnappers were actually in league with each other. Their plan had gone exactly as they had hoped. Smith had rescued the Royal Couple, but had supposedly been killed along with the soldiers in an explosion deep inside a cave system in the Derbyshire Peak District. Everyone had been happy. The government was happy that the Royal Couple had been saved, and just as happy that the problem of what to do with Smith had finally been taken out of their hands. Meanwhile Smith and his friends from The Brotherhood were content that they had escaped with not only their lives, but also with six million pounds ransom money.

Now, the man once known to the world as John Smith is living in Norway under the name of Jarl Ericsson, and he has never been happier in his whole life. He has a nice home and a healthy bank balance that means he never has to work again. But most of all he has the love of a good woman who is his equal in all things. Linda is tough, resilient and very intelligent, as well as being a very good looking woman. She is his best friend as well as his lover and Jarl is a very happy man indeed. He has finally found the peace and quiet that he has craved - and for so long.

TWO

22nd August
Telemark, southern Norway

The moose was standing knee-high in the water of the shallow lake, his huge head with its massive set of palmate antlers regularly dipping down into the still waters. Each time his bulbous nose and pendulous upper lip rose from the water he had a mouthful of fresh green lily stems which he proceeded to chew and swallow with obvious enjoyment and relish. He was a magnificent animal, standing well over two metres at his shoulder, with a body length of over three metres. He probably weighed in excess of eight hundred kilograms and it was easy to see why people often died when they accidentally drove into one of these animals on dark nights on the Norwegian roads. It must be like driving into a solid brick wall.

  Jarl Ericsson lay very still in the tall green-turning-gold grass that lined the top of the steep, almost vertical bank of the lake, barely thirty metres from the huge beast. Though it had taken him and Linda the best part of an hour to crawl so close to the moose, Jarl still found his eyes drawn from the almost primeval sight of the feeding animal back to the face of his companion. Doctor Linda Webb was a very beautiful woman and he couldn't resist soaking up her features as she lay there in the warmth of the early morning sun, looking down on the magnificent beast below them. Linda had been a renowned cardiothoracic surgeon until about a year ago. She was five feet six inches tall, with a slim and athletic body, despite the fact that she was past her half century, and had a sharp, inquiring mind.

"Why doesn't he notice us?" she asked him in a whisper, turning slightly so that she could look into his eyes. "We're so close to him. Surely all he has to do is look up and he'll see us here?"

Jarl smiled at her.

"It's a sort of unwritten law," he replied. "Animals, and that includes humans, tend to think in just two dimensions. They will look *around* them to search for danger, but they *never* look up."

"Surely that can't be true?"

"I know it sounds daft, but it's true, honest! I'll give you an example. When I was a young soldier we used to train for all sorts of situations and one of them was how to clear a wood of the enemy. The way that we do it is with two rows of soldiers moving forward in extended line, one line about ten metres behind the other. The first line has the majority of the men in it and they do what comes naturally to them. They move forward slowly checking out bushes, and hollows in the ground for hidden enemy, ready to open fire as soon as they spot something suspicious. The second line has fewer men in it and their task is purely to look up and search the trees. You see, we'd found out from bitter experience that just one line of men would search at ground level very thoroughly, but would always miss a clever enemy that had climbed upwards into the trees. They'd just pass beneath them without looking up!"

Linda's look was quizzical.

"That's still hard to believe," she said and Jarl smiled at her look.

"I know it is, but believe me its true - *they never look up!*"

At this moment, as they were lying together so close that they were almost touching, and with Linda's face slightly flushed with the excitement of the stalk, she looked the most gorgeous woman in the world to Jarl. He could not resist the temptation he had been feeling for quite a while now and reached out to grab her and pull her closer, rattling the grass stems as he did so. Linda giggled when she saw the look that had come on to his face.

"What? Now?" she whispered, feigning surprise. Her Australian accent was still quite strong, even after years of working overseas, and that was yet another thing he loved about her.

"Yes. Now!" Jarl's voice had become husky with his rising need. Their bodies entwined and neither noticed the massive moose, startled by the sounds of their movement, as it bounded out of the lake and galloped away into the woods on the other side of the lake at top speed, the ground seeming to shake beneath its massive weight.

Life was good for Jarl Ericsson and Linda Webb. Linda had originally moved to Norway to further her career as a surgeon. However when the man she had first known as David Keller (the name he had taken while escaping from Africa) and then as John Smith had re-entered her life carrying a big bag of money, she had retired from her busy working life. It had been a huge shock for her when he came knocking on the door of her modest studio apartment in Bergen. At that time she had believed that he was dead.

She remembered hearing about his death on a Norwegian news broadcast when the British Prison Service had made an announcement that John Smith had died as the result of an accident whilst serving out his life sentence in Winson Green Prison. At the time she had been totally overcome by the intensity of her sadness, crying herself to sleep every night for over a month, mourning the man that she had fallen in love with while he had been her patient. In her deep, dark despair she had been more miserable than she had ever been in her life before. It had been bad enough that John had been sentenced to life for a crime that she was completely certain he had not committed. But at least he had still been alive, and where there was life there was always hope, no matter how slim.

Smith had become world famous after he fought and killed eight Islamic terrorists who hijacked the aircraft flying from The Gambia to London. His bravery had saved the lives of all the crew and passengers but had also prevented the terrorists from crashing the plane into Buckingham Palace. Thus he had also saved the entire Royal Family from almost certain destruction as they had gathered together to celebrate the Queen's birthday.

The critically injured man was at first hailed as a hero around the world. There were even plans to honour him with a Victoria Cross for his bravery. But then the world changed its mind about him after it became widely known that he had once been an assassin working covertly for the British government. People's attitude towards him changed as time passed. They began to call him an assassin and murderer, rather than the life-saving hero that he was. But by then Linda was already falling in love with the quiet, troubled man. She had seen his cold, murderous side in the video of his fight with the terrorists that had been filmed by a BBC cameraman who had sat next to him on the flight. But she had also seen the other side of him, the gentle side that was frightened of talking to his own estranged sons because he was worried about what they might think of him. She had never met such a complex man in her life before and she had missed him terribly when he had been imprisoned.

Then he had turned up on her doorstep, half of his face hidden by a huge bandage where he had had plastic surgery to remove a nasty scar acquired in the fight with the terrorists. She had recognised the black eyes, handsome face and gravelly voice immediately and had almost fainted with shock. Once she'd recovered and Smith had explained everything that had happened, including the setting up of the Royal Couple's mock kidnapping, she had felt a huge wave of love and happiness wash over her. There was never a doubt in her mind. She was going to spend the rest of her life with this man, no matter what.

THREE

Telemark, southern Norway

Linda Webb gave up her job in a local hospital the day after Smith turned up at her home. Together they figured that they had a million and a half pounds between them, counting Jarl's share from the ransom money and Linda's own savings. She also had a fair-sized pension fund set up which would bring in enough money for them both to live off, even though she was retiring earlier than planned.

They left Linda's rented studio apartment in Bergen and moved south to Stavanger, a small city on the south-western coast of Norway. There they paid cash for a detached house on the island of Hundvåg. Although the house faced the North Sea, it was sheltered from the worst of the winter weather by the bulk of the Stavanger Peninsular. Neither John nor Linda were city folk though, and after a month or two of getting to know each other, they decided to buy a second summer home in the Norwegian countryside so that they could get away on their own.

After a few months of searching they settled on an old white painted wooden farm house situated in a lush green valley in the village of Flatdal. The village consisted of a couple of dozen houses, most of them with the typical grass-covered 'green' roofs of Norway. Flatdal is in the county of Telemark about one hundred and twenty miles east of Stavanger as the crow flies. The countryside there is fantastic and everywhere they looked there was magnificent scenery of high mountain crags covered in dark green pine and spruce forests. They moved into their summer retreat at the end of May and found that they were slightly early as most of the land was still covered in deep snow. They didn't care though as they were in each others company. As the months had come and gone their love for each other had passed its initial 'honeymoon' period and was slowly growing into a deeper understanding and feeling for each other, making each moment spent together even happier than the last.

Linda surprised Smith with her deep knowledge of nature and the countryside. As the snow slowly disappeared, except for that which remained on the highest mountain peaks, they spent most of their time wandering in the mountains around their new home and searching out the wildlife. Linda knew the name of every butterfly, dragonfly, wild flower, bird and animal that they came across, and slowly Jarl, who had spent most of his own adult life in one wilderness after another, came to recognise and love them too. There was a wealth of wildlife in the forests and traditionally-managed hay meadows of Telemark, from the golden fritillary butterflies that floated across the flowery meadows, through to the rough-legged buzzards that circled above them on lazy wings. They explored the rivers and streams together, watching with fascination the secret work of labouring beavers in the twilight hours and the leaping antics of salmon making their way upstream to breed. They lay in the summer sunshine together in high meadows full of brightly coloured sedums and scabious, and searched through the thick conifer forests for brief sightings of the rare and elusive white-backed woodpeckers and pine martens. It was, quite simply, the most perfect time of both of their lives and they thoroughly enjoyed every minute of it spent together.

For his part, Smith proceeded to teach Linda some of the skills that he had learned in a lifetime spent as a Special Forces soldier. He taught her to use the 'ghost walk', and 'monkey' and 'leopard crawls' to stalk close to deer and beaver, and he taught her how to survive in the wilderness. By August she knew how to filter water from puddles to drink using a pocket-lining, build a lean-to shelter out of tree branches, light a fire using nothing but flashlight batteries and wire wool, and how to set improvised traps to catch animals for food. They laughed and loved their way through summer days of walks in the mountains and evenings in candlelight and making love. Slowly it dawned on both of them that they had at last found their soul-mate.

FOUR

22nd August
Telemark, southern Norway

They returned to their new home in the early evening, a few hours after stalking the moose. The old farmhouse was quiet and peaceful in its valley and all was well with the world. Then the peace was shattered – Linda's mobile telephone rang.

They didn't receive many calls so when the strident sound of the mobile broke into the peace and quiet they both nearly jumped out of their skins. It was Linda who answered:

"Hello."

"Is that Linda Webb? *Doctor* Linda Webb?"
It was a woman's voice on the other end of the crackly line.

"Yes, that's right. Who's this?"

"You probably won't remember me, Doctor. My name is Helen Wright. We've met once, but only briefly, at the East Surrey Hospital in Redhill."

"Oh, you're right. I'm afraid I don't remember you. Were you a patient? How did you get this number?"
Linda's voice tightened up at the mention of the hospital where she had met her lover. John noticed the change in her tone and wandered over towards her, worried.

"I'm sorry, Linda, but you don't have much time. It's very important that I talk to *John Smith*. Is he there?"
Linda frowned over at her partner, suddenly very, very

frightened.

"John Smith? I'm afraid that you're mistaken, Miss Wright. I don't know anyone by that name."

Smith's antennae perked up at the mention of his name. *What the hell?* he thought, moving close to Linda so that he could listen in on the conversation. Linda held the mobile between their heads so he could hear better, a look of intense fear beginning to grow on her face. The voice on the other end of the line suddenly became harder and more forceful.

"John? Are you there, John? It's urgent that you talk to me, John. I'm Detective Sergeant Helen Wright. I used to work with DCI Davies of the Serious and Organised Crime Agency. Linda, is John there? I must speak with him urgently! Please!"

Smith took the mobile gently from Linda's hand.

"Hello, Helen," he said quietly.

"Thank God! John, I know that this call must be setting off all sorts of alarm bells in your head, but I haven't got time to go into too many details. They're coming for you, John! They're already on their way! You must get out of there!"

"Calm down, Helen. Who's coming? What's going on?"

It was Davies of course, Detective Chief Inspector Alan Davies. He was the British policeman who had ruthlessly hunted down John Smith once before. Davies had never believed that Smith had died in the Peak District explosion and he had kept searching for him out of pure bloody-mindedness. When he had heard that Doctor Webb had left the East Surrey Hospital he found out where she had moved to in Norway and had hired a private detective to check her out. He thought that there was a slim chance that Smith might have gone into hiding with her. She had been much too protective of Smith in the hospital and he believed that there was more to their relationship than a simple doctor-patient thing.

"Jesus, John, you've got to get out of there! Now!"

"Why, Helen? Who's coming for me?"

Armed only with a couple of grainy photographs of a man that vaguely *looked* like Smith, Davies had been faced with disbelief and disinterest by his colleagues in the police. Somehow he had got in touch with the Iranians, who still had a *fatwa*, a 'death-notice', on Smith and had travelled to Norway with them. After searching Smith and Linda's house in Stavanger, Davies and the Iranians had found out that they were spending the summer in Telemark. But Davies was scared to death of his new-found Iranian 'friends', and had decided to call Helen and tell her what was going on before they left for Telemark. He hoped that the knowledge of the phone call to a colleague would help to protect him from the Iranians if anything went wrong. But Helen had been shocked to the core by the call. She broke into Davies's office and had found the report from the private detective which included Linda's mobile number.

"You must get out of there, John!"
Smith's voice was hard.

"Okay, Helen. Don't worry, we'll get out of here. Thanks. But why, Helen? Why warn us about Davies?"
He couldn't hide his cynicism.

"It doesn't matter, John! Just get out of there. Please!"

"Okay, Helen." He hung up, his soldier's mind already fast-forwarding into what they must do and how. He looked at Linda's face, white now with fear despite her summer tan. "Linda, we'd better do as she says and get out of here. I don't know why she's called or whether she's telling the truth, but we ought to move and move fast. We can figure it out later when we're safe."
He held her gently by the shoulders and looked deeply into her eyes.

"Sort out some food quickly. Get enough for a couple of days in the bush. Tins and packets only, things that we can eat cold and uncooked if we have to."
When she didn't move he pulled her close and held her tight for a moment. He could feel her shaking with fear

against him.

"Why's this happening?" she almost sobbed. "Why *now*, John, after all this time?"

"I don't know, Linda, but we *will* find out, I promise you. Let's just get out of here first. Go and get the food, okay? I'll sort out our kit."
He pushed her gently in the direction of the kitchen.

"Make it quick though love, okay?"
She nervously returned his reassuring smile as she went.

FIVE

22nd August
Telemark, southern Norway

For all of his adult life John Smith had either been fighting or preparing to fight, often for his life. Being prepared for anything, especially for the unexpected, was just another part of his training. Therefore it wasn't that surprising that he could immediately lay his hands on two rucksacks, one for him and one for Linda, already packed and awaiting an emergency such as this. Such careful forethought had saved his bacon many times in the past, and since he had been 'on the run' it had become perhaps even more important than when he had been a soldier. The rucksacks contained everything that he could think of which they might need in a hurry – sleeping bags, one-man bivvies, folding stoves and solid Hexamine fuel blocks, water bottles, spare clothing, waterproofs, flashlights, binoculars, multi-tools, first-aid kits, survival kits, washing kits, even a civilian nightscope which they often used to watch nocturnal wildlife in the brief hours of Norwegian darkness. His rucksack also had a few spare passports and driving licences in different names hidden away in its lining. These were a part of his legacy from working with the British Secret Intelligence Service. They were genuine documents that he stringently kept up to date in case they were needed, and they were totally untraceable. The only thing that he didn't have in the rucksack - and which he bitterly regretted now - was a firearm. He had desperately hoped that his need for a gun for self-defence had passed. There were a couple of long and stout-bladed Bowie knives though. They would be useful for other things besides chopping firewood and skinning rabbits - like killing.

Smith moved quickly around the farmhouse gathering up their jackets and boots. He knew that they only had a couple of hours of light left and that the night would be very short, Norway being so far north of the equator.

His mind went over everything that Helen Wright had told them.

I should have killed that bastard Davies when I had the chance, he thought. *Next time, I will. Who are these bloody Iranians? How many of them are there? What are they armed with? How long before they get here?*

Linda brought the food from the kitchen and together they stowed it into their rucksacks. Then they put on their hiking boots and jackets. As they left the house, Smith paused for a few seconds before locking the door. He could easily set up a booby trap for his unexpected visitors. He could make simple explosives out of half a dozen common ingredients that were found in most houses and kitchens, but it would take valuable time, and anyway, he loved this old farmhouse. Smith had never been so happy anywhere in his life before and he'd be buggered if he was going to destroy it just to knock a few bloody religious fanatics on the head.

They jumped into their old Land Rover which was parked out the front and started it up.

The village where they lived was spread out over quite a distance along the valley, with separate minor roads going off in different directions towards small groups of houses. Their house lay at the foot of the mountains along the western edge of the valley, in a small group with two or three other houses, at the end of a long tarmacked road wide enough for only one vehicle.

As Linda drove the Land Rover at breakneck speed, John was peering ahead through the windscreen.

"Shit!" he suddenly shouted. "Stop, Linda! Stop!" She slammed on the brakes and the old four-by-four shuddered to a halt in a cloud of dust and smoke.

"What is it?"

There was a note of panic in her voice as she followed his gaze. There was no need for Smith to answer as she immediately saw the vehicles advancing rapidly towards them along the road. There were at least two dark-coloured cars about a quarter of a mile away. Linda immediately slammed the Land Rover into reverse gear and accelerated.

"What are you doing?" asked Smith.

"There's a track that leads off into the woods. We should be able to make it!"

The engine of the Land Rover whined in outrage as she reversed quickly and smoothly up the road, her eyes glued to the wing mirrors. There was only one fork behind them in the road, and that was just an entrance to a dirt farm track going south and then west towards the mountains across half mile or so of cultivated land. As they passed the fork Linda stamped her foot on the brakes and they skidded to a stop, then she slipped the Land Rover into first gear and they drove forward onto the farm track. The approaching cars were much closer now, having chewed up the separating distance, but the Land Rover spurted forward, bouncing over the uneven track surface as it raced along.

"When we get to the end don't stop Linda, just drive straight through the gate, even if it's closed, and then keep on going up the track into the forest. We won't be able to get too far up the track, but we'll get further up than those bastards behind us will be able to and it'll give us a better head start."

As Linda accelerated and smashed through the closed wooden gate with grim determination written on her face, Smith leant over to blindly grab the rucksacks off the back seat so they were ready to go with the minimum of delay. He swore as his hand was stabbed by a six-inch nail lying loose on the back seat. It had fallen out of a half-empty packet of nails that he had used to fix an old rickety fence a few days before. With a tight smile on his face, already thinking well ahead, he picked up the packet and shoved it into his jacket pocket.

The track led up a steep incline between rows of mature spruce trees covering the hillside in a thick green blanket, gradually narrowing and getting rougher until it became just a footpath with the trees towering above and around it. Linda drove the vehicle upwards until it just couldn't go any further. Then they jumped out, shouldered their rucksacks, and started up the path on foot. In the sudden silence they could hear distant shouting and the sound of car doors slamming shut below them.

The past few months spent wandering around the mountains had hardened their muscles and kept them both pretty fit. They drove themselves up the footpath at a good pace, with Smith constantly looking over his shoulder for a sign of pursuit. His brain was trying to figure out their best course of action to get the bastards off their tail. He quickly came to a decision.

"Listen, Linda, I think we can afford to slow up slightly." He was pleasantly surprised that they weren't out of breath despite the forced pace of their upward march. After all he wasn't a spring chicken anymore and neither was Linda. "Once we get to the top of this mountain the trees start to thin out and we'll have to decide which way to go from there. I know that there's a ridge line running north-westwards but it's got a road along it and it wouldn't surprise me if the Iranians get a vehicle up there ahead of us to cut us off." He adjusted the straps on his rucksack as they slowed their pace. "Do you remember that this path leads up to a steep scree slope at the top?"

"Yes", replied Linda, "and it's pretty open country once you cross the crest. They'll be able to see us from miles away."

"Yep. Except that it'll be dark in about an hour."

"I hadn't thought of that." She smiled as she looked

up into the evening sky. "We'll be able to lose them in the dark, won't we?"
Smith smiled back at her.
"I'm not sure that I want to," he said, a little grimly. "Not yet anyway."

SIX

22nd August
Telemark, southern Norway

Detective Chief Inspector Alan Davies was well pissed off. Nothing was going to plan, as usual.

He had been on a high for the past few months after finding out that John Smith was still alive and well and living with his fancy piece in Norway. Not one of his fellow officers had figured out what *he* had, that Smith had *not* died in an accident in Winson Green Prison. He still didn't know how the bastard had pulled it off. Maybe the Secret Intelligence Service had made a deal with their former agent or perhaps *The Sun* had put enough pressure on the Government after all and managed to wangle him a royal pardon. It didn't really matter to Davies. Smith was a convicted paedophile and as far as he was concerned, even if Smith had not actually committed the crime that he was sent down for, so what? He was still a murderer and a madman and he had fucked up Davies's career with his bloody rampage a couple of years ago. He'd made him look a complete tit in front of his colleagues and his bosses and Smith was going to pay for that.

Davies had once been the officer in charge of the Cambridgeshire Police Serious and Organised Crime Agency, but now, in his own mind at least, he was just another bloody 'plod' with the Child Protection Unit. The Child Protection Unit is divided into several teams that deal with different aspects of child abuse and protection. The top job within the unit is with the 'Major Investigation Team', which investigates child homicide and suspicious deaths of children. Then there is the 'Serious Case Team', which investigates the most complex child abuse cases, followed closely by the 'Paedophile Unit', which specialises in targeting child abuse online, including the grooming of children and the distribution of child pornography. But Davies had not been chosen by his superiors for any of these top teams. Instead he had been put in charge of the bloody 'Partnership Team'. This team spent its time 'engaging' with key stakeholders amongst other statutory and volunteer organisations and Davies absolutely hated the job. There was no chance of proving himself by investigating major crimes and no glory to be had. He spent all of his time in endless boring bureaucratic meetings with faceless people. Life was passing him by and he had been moved from the fast lane onto the hard shoulder, and all because of that fucker Smith!

Davies's fellow officers had grown tired of his obsession with John Smith. He had had to beg, borrow and steal the information that finally gave him Doctor Linda Webb's address in Stavanger. Even when he had hired that bloody expensive private detective to follow Webb, and he had come up with a couple of grainy photographs of Smith, still no one believed him. But he had known that the man in the photos had been Smith.

It was bloody obvious! Yet they still did not believe him! How could they have their own noses so far up their arses that they couldn't see the truth? Shit, he'd show the bastards that he was right!

That was when it had dawned on him. Even though they could see that he had finally found Smith, no one was interested. As far as they and the rest of the world were concerned, Smith was dead and buried. None of them wanted to be involved in another manhunt that would only give them grief. It could affect their careers just as badly as it had Davies's and not one of them wanted that. They wanted bugger all to do with it, or with Davies either.

Spineless bloody wankers, the lot of them!

For a while Davies had fantasised about killing Smith himself. He thought about buying a hunting rifle with a telescopic sight and putting a bullet into his head, just like Smith had done to his former SIS handler, Harry. But he was a shit shot, even with a pistol, and he knew it. What he really needed was a bloody great machine gun, like the one Rambo used in his films. He might have a chance of hitting Smith then, so long as he was only a few feet away and didn't move a lot. Fat chance of that! He thought about getting up close to Smith and using a knife on him, but then he remembered, with a shiver down his spine, the video that had shown Smith taking on and killing eight terrorists armed with knives. He knew that he wouldn't stand a chance against that bastard. He'd end up like a slice of beef steak at a barbeque, minus the sauce, but with a side order of his own blood, snot and gore. He fantasised about putting a bomb under Smith's car and blowing him up. But he knew nothing about explosives and wouldn't have a clue about where to get hold of any, even if he had. He looked up recipes for bomb-making ingredients on the internet, but then had a vision of it all going wrong and a home-made bomb blowing up in his own face. He'd find it hard to pick his nose with no fingers left. He racked his brains for ages about how to take down his nemesis. He even considered going back to the SIS and giving them the information that he had on Smith, but he knew that they would keep him out of the loop as soon as he handed it over, and he wanted more than anything in the world to be there when the bastard finally got what he deserved.

Finding a way of taking his vengeance on Smith had filled his every waking hour.

Even in his sleep he dreamed about it and the only person he could talk to about the whole mess was his once close colleague, formerly Detective Constable, now Detective Sergeant, Helen Wright. He knew that she had once had a crush on him, but like a fool he had never followed it through and fucked her. Now she even showed disdain when he constantly phoned her up at her home or visited her in her new role in the National Wildlife Crime Unit. *Wildlife crime! What a bloody come down for her!* She had once been his right-hand woman in SOCA. *How the hell could she enjoy working for such a poxy bloody outfit as wildlife crime? Jesus!* She listened to him though. In fact she was the only one that did, despite not even liking him anymore.

Then, one day, as he was going through his file on Smith for the thousandth time, it suddenly dawned on him. The *fatwa* - the Death Notice that had been served on Smith by some Iranian religious leader after he had killed those Muslim terrorists on board the aircraft. Surely the Iranians would be interested in finding out that Smith was still alive. They wouldn't fuck about, would they? They'd be straight in and knock the bastard off! Perfect! And wasn't there something said about a reward of half a million pounds?

It hadn't been that easy though. Davies had made contact with an Iranian named Farad Pahlavi who he'd got to know of during his time with SOCA. He'd been an alleged member of a criminal gang that smuggled drugs across Europe from Afghanistan, but they had found fuck all to charge him with. The only lead they had had on the case was from an informer inside the organisation. But after Pahlavi had been arrested the informer had disappeared - presumably murdered - and they had had to let Pahlavi walk free. Davies remembered though that there had been talk about Pahlavi possibly being a member of MISIRI, the Iranian Military Intelligence Agency, but again they could find no evidence against him.

Davies had sought out Pahlavi, meeting him in a seedy coffee shop in Soho. He had shown his file on Smith to the Iranian but the man had laughed in his face, saying that he was bonkers for thinking that he had anything to do with Iranian intelligence. Davies had finally left the coffee shop, absolutely fuming at how the bloody Iranian had taken the piss out of him and his wild ideas, convinced that the man was nothing but a crook.

Then, about a week later, Davies had been approached by a man on the street. The man had shoved a handgun into Davies's belly and ordered him into a Mercedes car, where he had found himself sitting with three hard-looking dusky-skinned men. They had remained silent and had refused to answer his questions and Davies had been scared to death. He was sure that he was going to be murdered, but instead the car had taken him to a well-appointed house in Kensington. The men had led him into a study lined with leather-bound books and rich furnishings. There he had talked to a well-dressed Iranian who had pumped him for every bit of information that he had found out about Smith. Davies had given the information freely but held back on two vital pieces - that Smith was living in Norway and his precise address. After an hour or so of negotiation he had finally struck a deal with the Iranian. He would be allowed to accompany the team that would be sent to kill Smith.

Davies wanted to be there at the end, to see that bastard finally get the fate that he so richly deserved. He would be there at the kill.

Davies had been summoned back to the house three weeks later and had been introduced to another Iranian called Hassan. Hassan was a tall, lean Persian with a hard face. He had coal-black eyes that reminded Davies of Smith, and the same total confidence in his own ability that Smith had always shown. Hassan had the attitude and demeanour of an ex-military of some kind and Davies had been drawn to him, knowing that he had finally met someone who would be able to match his nemesis. It was with a happy heart that he had listened to the man's plans.

The following morning Davies had caught the regular ferry service from Newcastle to Stavanger, and once in the Norwegian city he had been picked up by Hassan and his team of killers, eight of them in total. Just like their leader they were a tough-looking bunch and Davies had once again been afraid for his life. What if they decided to just use his information and discard him, probably with a bullet in the back of his head? He had suddenly realised just how deep a hole he had dug himself with his obsession about Smith. For the first time he was really sorry that he had got involved in this craziness, but it was too late to back out now. He had gone with the team to Linda Webb's house on the coast of the Island of Hundvåg, where the Iranians had stormed the secluded place in true military style, weapons bristling. Davies didn't know whether to be angry or relieved that Smith and his fancy woman weren't there.

The men had systematically searched the house from top to bottom and had soon found the legal papers relating to the purchase of the farm house in Telemark. It was an easy assumption to make that the house at Flatdal was a summer residence and that Smith and Webb would be there.

Davies had not been threatened at any time by any of the Iranians but he still felt afraid for his own life, and that was why he had slipped away and phoned Helen Wright to let her know where he was and what was happening. Afterwards he told Hassan about making the call. He thought of it as insurance and told the Iranian that if he didn't return unharmed, after the mission to kill Smith was over, then a colleague of his had been informed about Hassan and his boss in Kensington. He told him that the information would be used to hunt the men down. Hassan simply smiled and shrugged his shoulders. He wasn't the kind of guy to be intimidated by a policeman, especially a stupid British policeman.

SEVEN

22nd August
Telemark, southern Norway

There had followed a hard, fast drive eastwards across the mountains of southern Norway for Davies and the Iranians. The landscape they travelled through was magnificent, with tall craggy mountains on every turn, some of them still covered in snow despite it being late summer and fairly hot and sunny. At some points the road even went through deep cuttings of ten to fifteen feet of hard-packed snow that had lain there all year.

    Davies had never been to Norway before and he was amazed at how immense the landscape was and at how few people there were in it. In fact they only passed one car going in the opposite direction in the whole four hours that it took them to get to Telemark.

    There weren't too many roads and they had followed the main E134 for most of the drive, so map reading hadn't been a problem. Their convoy of two dark blue BMWs ate up the distance. They eventually left the main road and turned west on to *Flatdalsbyen*, a minor road that took them into the village of Flatdal itself. At this point they were stumped for a while as none of the houses had names or numbers on them. They had no idea where to find the farmhouse that Smith and Webb had bought.

    Hassan finally found out where the house was located by asking the Lutheran priest at *Flatdal Kyrkje,* the village church. The smiling young priest had pointed out the road that they must take to get there. However, unfortunately for him, his open friendliness began to turn to suspicion when he eyed the two cars full of dark-skinned, tough-looking men. Hassan solved any potential problems by steering the priest back into the church with a hand on his elbow and then putting a bullet into the back of his head from a silenced pistol. He then quickly hid the body in the vestry. Within minutes the vehicles had turned around and were zooming north again. They then turned at speed on to *Kvålevegen*, the road that led to the farmhouse.

Davies didn't know that Hassan had murdered the priest, but he was so exhilarated by this stage that he probably wouldn't have cared anyway. His prey was within sight now. Hassan swore out loud as they drove along and pointed out the rapidly reversing Land Rover in front of them on the road. It was obviously trying to get away and that meant only one thing: somehow Smith and his girlfriend had been warned. Hassan swore again as he saw the Land Rover turn off the road on to a rough farm track and then began to pick up speed. He turned to follow but had to reduce his own speed as his low-slung BMW saloon wasn't built for this type of terrain. The last thing he wanted to do was to rip the bottom out of it on the rock-strewn track. The Land Rover spurted forward towards a thick plantation of trees that carpeted the steep slope ahead. He watched it as it smashed through a wooden gate and started up the incline. Then it was lost to sight amongst the trees.

Hassan's BMW, with the other car following, eventually made it through the gate and started on up the hill after the fugitives. But it was only a few hundred metres before the road got a lot rockier and began to peter out. Hassan pulled to a halt. It took another ten minutes or so before his team had organised themselves for the pursuit, removing small bergens from their cars and pulling on hiking boots. Like good soldiers anywhere, his team had come well prepared for any contingency. They listened as they got ready and were disturbed to hear the Land Rover's engine still climbing for some distance above them. Smith had got himself a good head start and it was getting longer by the minute, but Hassan reined in his impatience and made sure that all of his team were ready. A quick look at a map of the area showed that the road they had initially taken through the village carried on northwards for a while and then looped westwards. It was possible that the fugitives were going to head towards it in the hope of finding help, so Hassan dispatched two of his men in one of the BMWs to patrol the road. He would keep in touch with them by using the small radio sets that they had brought with them. When everyone was ready they set out to climb the mountain in pursuit.

EIGHT

22nd August
Telemark, southern Norway

This was the point at which Davies found himself completely pissed off. Nothing was going to plan. This was supposed to have been a quick visit for him into Norway. Just a short trip into Stavanger and *bam*, Smith and his smartarse girlfriend were going to be dead. Now he found himself halfway across bloody Norway, following a bunch of very fit Iranian hitmen as they pounded up the forested slope of a bloody steep mountain. After only ten minutes of keeping up with the Iranian's punishing pace he had begun to flounder, realising that he was, after all, just a short-arsed copper with a bit of a beer belly, who hadn't done any serious fitness training for bloody years. He started to lag behind. His breath was rasping through his throat, he had a painful stitch in his side and his legs were beginning to feel like he was wearing lead boots. Vaguely he remembered his youth, when he had been full of vim and energy: how far away those days seemed to him now. He'd spent the last ten years sitting behind a desk. Until Smith had fucked up his life, his one 'sporting' activity had been the weekly poker game with the lads from SOCA, and the only exercise he had got was from lifting of a pint of lager to his mouth. Nowadays, doing a five-fingered shuffle while watching porn on the internet was the only cardio-vascular exercise that he took, and that never lasted more than a minute or two.

Davies watched the Iranians pounding up the track ahead of him with envy and hatred. *Bloody rag-headed wogs!* his thoughts screamed at him. The Iranians seemed to bounce forward with every step while his legs felt like jelly that hadn't set properly, threatening to fail completely and send him pitching head-first into the ground. *Uncivilised savages!* he thought, as he saw them looking back and grinning at his plight, totally ignorant of the fact that the Persians had a culture going back thousands of years and had once governed an empire of 'superpower' proportions, while his own people had still been living in mud huts.

Thankfully the Iranians slowed right down when they spied the abandoned Land Rover up ahead, and then they stopped. Some of them stayed on the track and prepared to give covering fire while Hassan and a couple of the others slithered off silently into the trees on the left of the track and cautiously went forward to look into the vehicle. It gave Davies a chance to bend down with his hands on his knees and noisily get his breath back. He just managed to refrain from bringing up his lunch.

When Hassan finally gave the signal that the Land Rover was safe, the Iranians moved on again. This time though, they moved more slowly and Hassan sent a couple of the men about fifty metres ahead of the main party to act as scouts and trackers. The rest of the men quartered the ground around them with their eyes as they marched on, constantly swinging the muzzles of their silenced machine-pistols from side to side, each of them covering their own arcs of fire. It suddenly dawned on Davies that they were hunting Smith now, in the sort of terrain that an old Special Forces soldier like him would be very comfortable in. For the first time Davies didn't only fear his Iranian comrades and what *they* might do to him, he began to fear what *Smith* might do too.

Shit! he thought. *What the fuck have I got myself into?* But it was too late for self-recriminations. He was fucked now and he knew it.

NINE

22nd August
Telemark, southern Norway

The light was beginning to fade when Smith first got a glimpse of his pursuers. Two tall, lean Iranians broke cover where the tree line ended and the steep scree slope began, just beneath the crest of the mountain. They moved forward cautiously, first one while the other prepared to give covering fire, then swapping roles. Smith smiled to himself as he lay hidden from view just below the crest.

Good, he thought. *Professionals. These must be scouts.*

Smith always preferred to be set against professionals rather than bloody amateurs. For one thing pros always acted within certain parameters. Parameters that had been learned the hard way. For example, they wouldn't rush unless they had too. Every act would be carried out cautiously because although they wanted to complete their mission and complete it well, they also wanted to be able to go home alive at the end of it. Bloody amateurs would often go off half-cocked and were unpredictable and therefore potentially more dangerous. Another good thing about pros was that they knew the score. They were hunting Smith and Linda and they would expect to take casualties. It was just a part of the job. They wouldn't moan about losing men. In a perverse sort of way this made Smith happier. He could kill them without feeling guilty.

The two Iranian scouts continued to leapfrog forward

below Smith, unaware of his presence. Behind them the rest of the team began to emerge from the tree line and follow the scouts on to the narrow pathway. Smith checked them over carefully through his binoculars, being careful to shield the lenses with his hands so that they wouldn't catch the sun and give his position away, looking around a rock rather than over it. He counted the men as they came out. There were six Iranians in total and Davies, easy to pick out as he sweated his way forward. He was dressed completely inappropriately in a light blue jacket more suited to an urban street than a bare mountainside. His companions were clothed in good quality olive-drab jackets made for walking in the mountains. They were armed to the teeth but Smith was glad to see that they didn't possess a long rifle. All they had were short-barrelled Mini-Uzi sub-machine-guns - which was great news as far as Smith was concerned. Although a Mini-Uzi can fire nine hundred and fifty 9mm rounds per minute on fully automatic, it has a barrel length of less than eight inches, meaning its effective range is only around one hundred metres. They would have to get close to Smith before they could use them with any accuracy. He would have been much less happy if one or more of them had carried a longer-barrelled assault rifle, or even worse, a bloody sniper rifle. Then he would really have been in trouble and he would have had to guard against being picked off from a decent range. He suspected that they all carried a pistol of some kind as a backup, but couldn't see them. Pros wouldn't be caught dead, if you'll excuse the pun, without some kind of backup.

As the Iranian soldiers - Smith couldn't help but think of them as soldiers now that he had seen how they operated - moved forward along the pathway below him, he searched in vain to spot their leader. This again was a sign that they were professionals. The leader would blend in well with the rest of the men so that he couldn't be taken out easily. Smith would have liked to see the leader of the men, but what the hell, he would no doubt get a chance to see him face to face before too long.

The slope between Smith and his hunters was very steep and covered in an unstable and dense layer of scree – loose chunks of rock ranging in size from small pebbles to football-sized lumps of sharp-edged granite. It was the perfect place for an ambush as there was no way that anyone could rush up that slope without setting off a landslide and losing their footing. They would have to move forward to the end of the pathway where it curled around the mountain crest before being able to attack an ambusher. Smith swore at himself once again for not having a firearm of some sort. He could have done real damage to his pursuers if he did have one.

Ah well, he thought. *I'll just have to make do with what's at hand. Improvisation is the name of the game.*

Smith risked a quick peek behind him over the crest line to make sure that he could still see where Linda was in the growing twilight. She was about half a mile past the crest and making her way downwards into the valley behind. He made a mental note of her position and how to reach her then turned back to the job in hand. He would have loved to take out that prat Davies, but at this point in the game it was obvious that the unfit, useless bastard was going to be more of a hindrance than a help to the Iranians, so he decided to leave him until later. Anyway, he wanted to be able to look the bastard right in the eye when he killed him. That would be much more satisfying.

Smith selected a large rock lying beside him, got a good grip on it and prepared to move. He picked out a likely-looking target below him. Then moving fast, he stood up, lifted the football-sized rock high above his head, aimed, and hurled it down the slope as hard as he could.

The fourth Iranian along in the main group of men glanced up as he heard a sound above him but he didn't have time to duck or move away from the well-aimed rock that caught him square on the top of his head. The chunk of heavy granite met his skull with a dull *thunk,* caving in the side of his skull and tumbling his lifeless body down the mountainside.

As soon as he had thrown the rock, and without waiting to see whether or not he had hit his target, Smith crouched down again behind cover and began to lob smaller rocks down on to the steep scree slope below him.

A few of the Iranians reacted to the attack on them very quickly and sprayed the top of the crest with short bursts of 9mm rounds, not knowing exactly where their attacker was, just knowing that he was above them.

The rocks that Smith threw down hit the scree slope and started small mini-avalanches which began to grow in size as more and more rock began to slide down the slope. Within seconds it seemed as though the whole slope was on the move as tons of rocks slid down towards the Iranians, raising a cloud of thick rock dust that billowed up as it went. The men saw what was happening and gave up their defensive fire. Instead they shouted to each other in alarm and began to run as fast as they could either back along the path or down off it on to the slope below. They threw themselves into cover behind anything that they could find, such as isolated trees or rock outcrops. Many of them were hit by the scree as it tumbled past them, but none of them seriously. After a couple of minutes the flow stopped and the dust began to settle. When they peered up at the crest of the mountain above them, it was empty.

Smith had gone.

TEN

23rd August
Telemark, southern Norway

Smith caught up with Linda about a mile from the ambush site. They laid up for a few hours in a tumble of rocks, getting some much needed rest. Smith was sure that the men following them would not continue to do so during the two or three hours of darkness, as they would not be able to follow their tracks. Unfortunately the ground was bare except for a few rock outcrops, with lots of exposed mud surrounding numerous small boggy pools. Even if he had been on his own Smith would have had trouble hiding signs of his passing; with the two of them it was hopeless.

While Linda slept, Smith kept a lookout, using the small nightscope that they had brought with them, just to make sure that they weren't caught unawares. He also used the time to dig a trench across the path where it narrowed to pass between two tall rock outcrops. It was fairly easy going, even though he only had a big Bowie knife to do the digging with, as the top nine inches or so was soft soil above the solid rock base. He carefully placed the spoil from the trench on to a spare shirt from his pack. Once he had finished digging and had made a trench about two feet long by eighteen inches wide and nine to ten inches deep, he deposited the spoil away from the spot and out of the sight of his pursuers. Next he retrieved the packet of six-inch stainless steel nails that he had earlier shoved into his pocket. He buried the heads of a few dozen of the nails in the trench so that they were vertical, with the needle-like sharp ends sticking up. Then he smiled grimly as he urinated on the nails. As the final touch he tore up the mud-soaked shirt he had used, laid a piece of the cloth across the trench (supporting its weight with a few sticks) and camouflaged it to look just like the rest of the path. He stepped back to look critically at the invisible trap.

Perfect.

This was one of the simplest booby traps that could be made. Known as a *'Punji stick pit'*, this type of booby-trap was first used by the *Kachins*, the mountain people of north-east Burma who fought against the British Indian Army in the 1870s, and it is from the *Kachin* language that the name *Punji* derives. However, *Punji* sticks were used to their greatest effect during the Vietnam War and had been a favourite weapon of the Vietcong against US forces. They were cheap, effective and could be made of almost any material, though most were simply sharpened out of slithers of bamboo or wood. They weren't only used in the bottom of pits, but were also placed out *in their millions* wherever US soldiers were likely to go, and they could easily be camouflaged in tall vegetation, water or even deep mud. The idea behind the use of a *Punji* stick pit wasn't as a killer trap (although large pits sometimes dug by the VC were aimed at killing any unfortunate US soldier that fell into them) – it was designed to slow the enemy down. When a soldier stood in a pit and his foot was painfully speared through by a *Punji* stick, he would first of all need to retrieve his foot from the pit, trying not to sustain more injuries - the VC often placed sticks in the side of the pit pointing down. Thus getting your foot out of one was often as painful as stepping in it in the first place. The injured man's foot would need to receive first aid treatment, then the unit involved would either be forced to reduce their pace for a man with a badly-injured foot (and possibly blood-poisoning as well), wait for the casualty to be evacuated by helicopter, or even abandon him altogether (not a good idea in *any* war, but especially when that war is against insurgents). The objective of Smith pissing on the nails that he used as *Punji* sticks was to give the recipient a dose of blood poisoning, and thus slow him down even more. The VC had used various poisons and toxins that they had rubbed on their *Punji* sticks, including frog poisons and their own excrement, but Smith didn't fancy a shit, so his urine would have to do.

Smith had first used *Punji* sticks during his time served in Afghanistan during the mid-1980s. The Soviets had had undisputed air superiority throughout their war with the Mujahedeen in Afghanistan at this time, and were able to move their troops around the theatre by helicopter with virtual impunity. Smith, fighting alongside the Muslim rebels against the Soviet 40th Army in the Panjshir Valley, had soon learned to sow hundreds of anti-personnel mines, along with thousands of *Punji* sticks in any spot that he considered could be used as potential helicopter landing points in and around the valley. This tactic had wounded dozens of Soviet troops, demoralising them as well as tying up many of their colleagues in looking after the wounded men, and considerably slowing down their operations in the area. He remembered well the lessons that he had learned the hard way during that bitter and brutal conflict.

As the light of the new day appeared on the horizon, Smith made himself and Linda a quick cuppa using the Hexamine stove. They drank it as they moved on and they ate a few oatmeal biscuits as breakfast as well. Smith had a feeling that this game would go on for a while and knew that they had to keep their strength up if they wanted to come out of it okay at the end.

Half a mile further on he told Linda to continue on without him for a while. He wanted to lie up and see if his trap did the job, then he'd catch her up later.

ELEVEN

23rd August
Telemark, southern Norway

    DCI Davies had spent a very uncomfortable few hours trying to get some sleep. Fortunately for him, the death of one of the Iranians had freed up the guy's sleeping bag for him to use. Unfortunately, it was so thin that it didn't keep the chill of the brief night from seeping into his bones and so he didn't sleep at all. It didn't help that he wasn't used to sleeping out in the 'wilderness' either. In fact he detested bloody camping – since he was a six-year-old and had had to sleep outdoors in his back garden. The absolute quiet of the Norwegian mountains had unnerved him horribly. He was more used to the sound of loud traffic and shouting drunks on the streets of home and he couldn't get the thought out of his mind that Smith was 'out there' somewhere, maybe even creeping up on him this very minute to bash his brains out with a rock. No, it was not a pleasant night at all.
    Strangely, his Iranian 'colleagues' had not seemed to be the least perturbed or angry that Smith had taken out one of their number so bloody easily the night before. They had simply stripped the body of anything that could be used to identify it and buried it in a shallow grave on the mountainside. Hassan had mumbled a few prayers over the grave in a language that Davies didn't recognise, and then had thrust the man's kit, including his jacket, boots and rucksack into Davies's hands. They were followed by the

man's Mini-Uzi and PC-9 ZOAF semi-automatic pistol (an unlicensed Iranian-made version of the Sig-Sauer P226).

"Do you know how to use these?" Hassan had calmly asked the policeman. Davies looked them over briefly before answering him more belligerently than he had intended:

"Of course I do. I was trained in the use of firearms by the Met!"

"Oh good," said Hassan, with just a tiny hint of sarcasm in his voice.

Then he ordered his sentries out to their positions and climbed into his own sleeping bag, which was much thicker than the one Davies had been given, the policeman noticed.

Davies should have felt much safer now that he was armed, but for some reason he suddenly felt more vulnerable carrying the guns and knowing that Smith was out there somewhere, waiting and watching.

Smith lay hidden by another outcrop of rocks as he watched the Iranians through his binoculars. They descended from the crest line where he had ambushed them the previous evening. The two scouts were out in the lead again, obviously following the tracks that had been left by Smith and Linda. The other men shook out into a loose arrowhead formation about fifty metres behind them as they hit the open country on this side of the mountain.

Smith lay down the binoculars and closed his eyes for a bit of a rest. A memory flashed into his mind of his first ever sergeant, when he had joined the British Army as a boy soldier in the Junior Leaders. The big Para sergeant had grinned at the faces of the frightened boys in front of him.

"You'll soon learn that there are a few golden rules that you must obey if you're going to survive in this man's army," he had said to them.

"The first rule you've probably already heard about: Never ever volunteer for anything."

A few of the boys nodded knowingly and the big man had grinned at them again.

"The second rule is that you eat anything what you can, whenever you can, because you never know when or where your next meal is likely to be."

"And the third rule is this: if you don't have to stand up; sit down. And if you don't have to sit down; then lie down. In other words: always conserve your energy until the moment when you'll really need it!"

Smith's face split into a huge grin at the memory, and then he dozed for a while.

Smith's well-trained body clock woke him up after twenty minutes. He raised his binoculars to his eyes and saw that the Iranians were close to where he had set his booby trap. The two scouts approached the part of the track where it narrowed by two tall piles of rocks on either side, and the lead man paused and went down on one knee. He carefully scanned the mountainside in front of him and then, signalling to his partner, he stood up and walked through the narrow opening.

Shit! thought Smith. *He's stepped over it. The lucky bastard!*

Smith tensed up as he watched the second scout approach the narrow bit of the track and time seemed to slow down for a second or two. He watched the man lift up his foot and place it down again on the ground, sure in his mind that this lucky bastard had also stepped over the trap.

Then the man leaned forward and put his bodyweight on to his leading foot. A howl of sheer agony escaped the man's lips as his foot slid down into the trench and the tips of the nails penetrated the soles of his boot and drove deep into his flesh.

Yes!

Smith watched with savage glee as the Iranian's carefully spaced formation broke up in disarray. None of the men knew what had happened to make their scout scream out loud, so they threw themselves to the ground and crawled into cover, not knowing what to expect next.

It took another twenty minutes before any sort of order had been redeemed from the disarray. The injured man had had the nails gently pulled out from his boot and then the boot had been removed by one of his colleagues, probably the team's medic, before he had bandaged the foot. Smith noted which one of the men was the medic and memorised the fact that he carried a larger rucksack than the others did. That information would no doubt be useful in the future.

The injured scout was obviously going to be of no use to the team from now on, as he could hardly put any weight on his bandaged foot without grimacing in pain. The medic gave him a few painkillers and the man was taken off point duty and replaced by someone else. Smith saw that the injured man was relegated to the rear of the team as they shook themselves out into formation again and moved on towards him. He also noticed that the medic had been ordered to carry the injured bloke's kit and help him to keep up with the others.

Interesting, he thought. *That'll probably provide the next part of today's entertainment.*

Smith crawled back from his position, and using the outcrop to hide himself from the Iranians he began to trot away from them. He ran with his arms down by his sides and his feet hardly lifting from the ground in the 'Mexican Shuffle'. Running in a relaxed manner like this he would eat up the distance between him and Linda with comparative ease and use up very little of his reserve energy. However, as he ran, his mind was actively working out his next move, the Iranian's likely response, and how he would deal with that in turn.

If he'd known how to play the game, John Smith might well have turned out to be very good at chess. The only trouble was that he enjoyed this type of game far more.

TWELVE

23rd August
Telemark, southern Norway

Sarhang (Colonel) Massoud Hassan had joined the *Artesh*, the Iranian Army, just six months before the end of the Iran-Iraq War in 1988. He was an orphan, as his father had been killed during the war while serving in the Iranian infantry. He had died during the notorious trench warfare that had been so horribly reminiscent of the war in Europe during the First World War. No one could tell Massoud exactly how his father had been killed, as there had been very few survivors of his regiment at the end. His mother had died of pancreatic cancer twelve months earlier and Massoud had become a fervent Muslim with an almost fanatical belief in his country and its Supreme Leader.

During his first two years' service in the Army, although he missed actually seeing combat during the war, Massoud showed a lot of promise as a soldier of *Allah* and as a leader, and was promoted three times, reaching the rank of *sarjukhe* (corporal). In 1988 his army unit was heavily involved in the Iranian government's infamous massacre of political prisoners. During this time Massoud's regiment secretly and systematically interrogated, tortured and then executed thousands of men and women. After carrying out this duty with enthusiasm he had been hand-selected by his superiors for the *Takavar*, a naval commando force. The following year was spent in training, first attending the physical training school for an intensive and muscle-wrenching eight weeks, followed by equally long and tough courses in sub-aqua diving, parachuting, weapons, unarmed combat, land warfare and finally close quarter combat.

At the end of his *Takavar* training Massoud served a six-month probationary term with an active combat unit, before becoming a fully-fledged commando. He had done so well during both his training and probationary periods that he was then commissioned as an officer with the rank of *sotvān yekom* (first lieutenant). He went on to serve with distinction in several conflicts, but most especially while operating with the Kurds against Saddam Hussein's regime in northern Iraq. His team specialised in small-unit raids involving sabotage, assassination and hostage-rescue.

In 2001, he volunteered to be transferred to the *Quds Force*, a special unit of the Iranian Revolutionary Guards, with the rank of *sarvān* (captain). This unit had been raised during the Iran-Iraq war and is considered by many international military analysts to be one of the best Special Forces units in the world, with extremely talented personnel. The *Quds Force* trains and equips foreign Islamic revolutionary groups around the Middle East. Most of Massoud's period of service with the unit was spent aiding and abetting the *Shi'a* death squads in Iraq and when he left he had attained the rank of *sargord* (major).

In 2007 he was transferred to the Ministry of Intelligence and National Security, which is Iran's leading intelligence-gathering agency. It has a covert arm reputed to recruit potential terrorists and plan international terrorist attacks, and is under the direct control of the Supreme Leader. Since 2010 he had served as an undercover intelligence officer at the Iranian Embassy in Oslo.

With over twenty five years of hard operational service behind him, Massoud was as intelligent and tough as they come. He was getting annoyed with the way that this mission was turning out though. It wasn't that he was emotionally attached to his men, in fact he considered them as simple 'dog soldiers' and had worked with only a few of them on previous missions before. He *was* annoyed at the apparent ease with which this infidel John Smith had killed one and injured another one of his men though. He felt that he was losing control of the situation, and that was what *really* annoyed him. He needed to regain the initiative or he knew that he would continue to take casualties and might be forced to face the unthinkable - failure. Failure was not an option in his position in the ministry and would most probably result in his imprisonment and eventual execution.

Massoud had a good idea of his opponent's past service for his own country and his high levels of skill, and Massoud was not a naive man. He knew that killing Smith would be hard, but he was supremely confident in his own skill and that he *would* succeed.

As the long day began to wane and with his team appearing to have got no closer to the man and woman they pursued (even though they had really pushed themselves), he decided to steal a march on them. As they had worked their way westwards down the bare slope of the valley, the landscape had begun to change again, becoming more wooded. The infidels had turned north about an hour ago on to a wide forest trail and were at last heading towards the road that ran along the top of the north-western ridgeline. Massoud was pleased that Smith and the woman had at last given him the opportunity to again seize the initiative. He contacted his two-man team, who were patrolling the ridgeline in their BMW, by radio. He ordered them to set up an ambush at the position that he was sure the infidels would reach the road. Instead of allowing his men a rest as the sun went down, he decided to risk pushing them forward in the darkness, hoping to be the hammer against his ambusher's anvil and to finally crush the enemy between them.

The British policeman, Detective Chief Inspector Alan Davies, was rapidly becoming another unwanted thorn in Massoud's side. The man was proving to be useless in the field, even though conditions were good. *Allah* alone knew when the man had last walked more than a mile at a time. He was completely unfit and was yet another factor in slowing his unit down. Even the soldier with the foot that had been injured by Smith's simple, but very effective, booby trap was marching faster that the British policeman. Massoud decided that if the policeman survived this night then his usefulness would be at an end. He would enjoy personally putting a bullet into Davies's head.

The thought of killing them all cheered Massoud up and he barked at his men to get them to move more quickly. The sooner that he could bring an end to this operation the better. He smiled at the prospect.

THIRTEEN

23rd August
Telemark, southern Norway

John Smith was also smiling. He was perched about twelve feet above the ground, well hidden in the branches of a pine tree and above the Iranians as they passed beneath him. He heard the third man in line bark an order at the others, presumably to force them on to a faster pace.

Ah, trying to steal a march on us eh? he thought. *Too bad for them that we're not going to stop for a rest tonight either. Does the Iranian commander think that we're stupid?*

As he patiently waited in his perch for the last of the Iranian line to pass beneath him, Smith suddenly had a flashback to the conversation he had had with Linda about forty minutes ago. When he had told her about what he was planning to do and how he was going to hide in the tree to carry it out, she had been horrified.

"But you'll be right above them, John! They've only got to look up and they'll see you easily!"

Smith had chuckled at her concern.

"Remember," he said. "They never look up! I'll be fine, I promise."

Smith shifted his weight and tensed his muscles as the last group of his pursuers walked beneath him. The group consisted of three men: Davies, the Iranian's medic and the injured man. They were separated from the main body of the enemy by about seventy metres. The last man was the medic, and he was the only one showing any sign of still being alert. Davies looked too knackered to lift his eyes off the ground in front of him, and the injured guy was in too much pain and discomfort, but the medic was looking left and right and every so often he would turn around as he walked, searching behind them and acting as a good tail-end Charlie should act.

Smith waited until the medic had passed beneath him, made sure that the man was looking forward and lowered himself from his branch, hanging a second by one hand before he dropped the short distance to the ground. Even the small noise that he made as he landed on the ground was enough to make the medic look around sharply. But Smith had expected this. With an ear-splitting yell intended to startle and disorientate, he charged forward across the three of four paces that separated them, a long and stout birch branch in his hand, sharpened to a point like a home-made spear.

The medic spun around, desperately trying to bring his weapon to bear on the terrifying apparition that materialised behind him. But he was too slow and Smith dodged past the man before driving the point of his spear deep into Davies's belly as he ran past him at full pelt. For Davies, those few short seconds seemed to slow down and last a lifetime. He saw Smith's grimly determined face as he dodged past the medic and drove the point of his spear deep into Davies's guts. Then Smith ran past him, dragging out the point of the spear and causing even more damage to the wound. Strangely, Davies felt no pain at first, just the numbing sensation that Smith had once again got the better of him. Then he stared down aghast at the ragged tear in his abdomen and began to scream as the pain hit him like a red hot poker. Bright red blood gushed from the torn flesh down on to his groin and his trousers.

Smith disappeared at speed into the thick woodland beside the track. The medic was the first of the group to come to his senses and he fired off a long sustained burst of rounds into the trees with his Mini-Uzi. But it was too little and too late. Smith had suddenly changed direction about ten metres into the trees and was out of sight of the Iranian. He had turned perpendicular to the track, and was already well away from where the Iranian expected him to be and to where he directed his firing. The screams of the wounded British policeman suddenly became much louder and more strident as Davies sank to his knees. He screamed until his throat was raw in his agony and fear.

Smith kept on running. He was safe from retribution and grinning at the screaming coming from behind him. He had spent some time carefully picking out a route to follow during his escape and had walked along it for a couple of hundred metres, removing any dead branches and other noisy obstacles on the ground so that he could run along it in silence. He remembered a mantra from the SAS, as he always did: Prior Preparation and Planning Prevent Piss-poor Performance. If circumstances allowed it was always worth the extra effort, no matter how tired, wet, cold or hungry you were, to spend some time imagining how the proposed action was going to go in your mind's eye. Smith would look at the ground he was going to go over, working out his future moves step by step and how the enemy would most likely react in turn to those actions. He would try out various scenarios in his mind until he decided on the one that had the most favourable outcome. Those few minutes of prior preparation and planning were often all that stood between him being successful and staying alive, or failing. Having a piss-poor performance was an option that he could never contemplate, because in his world failure meant death. Smith was the ultimate professional. That was why he was still alive while so many of his colleagues were dead.

FOURTEEN

23rd August
Telemark, southern Norway

Politibetjent (Police Inspector) Lars Gundersen of the National Criminal Investigation Service of the *Politi-og Lensmannsetaten* (the Norwegian Police Service) stooped down in the vestry of the Flatdal Church. *The body of the Lutheran priest had obviously been hidden in a hurry,* Lars thought, as he noticed how it had been more or less stuffed into a small cupboard, leaving a trail of blood across the floor. He groaned as he pushed himself back to a standing position, his leg bones cracking with the effort. He had had very little sleep during the past two days dealing with another murder in Notodden, a man who had killed his wife during a matrimonial argument. At least that one had been easy to solve though, especially as the husband had been the one to call the police, confessing to the killing almost immediately. This murder, on the other hand, appeared to be something entirely different, something much more sinister.

Lars sighed as he turned to Doctor Telma Carlsen, the forensic pathologist assigned to the case.

"Well? What do you make of it, Doctor?"
Even though Telma was covered from head-to-toe in a white barrier suit and wore a face-mask and gloves, he knew from previously working with her that she was a good-looking woman in her early forties. She sighed too as she answered.

"He was shot in the back of the head at close range by a low velocity handgun, probably a 9mm semi-automatic though I'll have to confirm that at the post-mortem of course. At first glance it looks like he was killed just inside the main door to the church and his body was then dragged into the vestry and shoved into this cupboard. The person who did it must have been in a hurry as they didn't make much of an attempt to clean up the blood trail."

"That's just what I was thinking. How long ago do you reckon, Doctor?"

"Well, I've taken several temperature readings from the body and they are approximately the same as the surrounding environment. Also the body is pliable, so *rigor mortis* has passed. The skin colour is quite pink in the lowest parts of the body, due to *hypostasis* or pooling of the blood, but there isn't any greenish tinge to the flesh yet, indicating that the time of death is less than forty eight hours ago. I would say that it is about twenty four hours since he died, but that's only a guess at this stage. I'll be able to narrow that down considerably once I get the body into the lab. Any ideas about who might have killed him?"

"One of the locals has reported seeing two dark-coloured cars outside the church late yesterday afternoon. She thought that she might have seen the priest talking to a dark-skinned man in drab clothes, but that's as far as we've got."

"Well I don't envy you your job Inspector. The killer could be anywhere in Norway by now."

"I know. I hate this sort of murder, I'd much rather have a clear-cut motive and a willing confessor."

He smiled at the pathologist for the first time since he had welcomed her on to the murder scene half an hour ago. Lars had been investigating serious crimes, including murder for many years now and he felt it was time to move on to something else within the police service. His enthusiasm for solving crimes was beginning to wane. Perhaps he would be able to get a desk job or something that would tide him over until his retirement in five years' time. He felt he was getting much too old for fieldwork these days. He sighed again.

The noise of the church door slamming open brought him out of his reverie with a lurch and he turned as a young police constable burst into the vestry.

"Inspector Gundersen!" the young man almost shouted in his excitement. "A neighbour has reported finding two abandoned cars! They're only about a mile and a half away!"

"Okay, lad, calm down. What make of cars?"
The constable made a conscious effort to slow down.

"One is a Land Rover, Sir, and the other is a BMW. I'm not sure what type, Sir."

"What colours are they?"

"The Land Rover is green, Sir, and the BMW is dark blue."

Lars paused as he put his thoughts together.

"Okay. It's just possible that the BMW might be involved in this murder. Let's go and have a look. Do you want to come along, Doctor?"

"No thanks, Inspector. I'd better stay here and wait for the coroner's vehicle. I'll need to supervise the removal of the body and make sure that evidence integrity is maintained. You know how useless these coroner's assistants can be!"

Lars smiled at the Doctor again.

"I do indeed, Doctor. I'll catch you later then."

Lars made his way out of the church. As he opened the door to his four-wheel drive Volkswagen Passat, his eye caught sight of his locked-down Heckler and Koch MP5 submachine gun and P30 pistol in their rack. *Let's hope I don't need to get permission to use them,* he thought.

FIFTEEN

23rd August
Telemark, southern Norway

Massoud was angry. Not only was he angry with that fucking Englishman John Smith for managing to lay a perfect ambush against his team and then to disappear into the forest like a fucking ghost, he was also angry at the stupid fucking British policeman, Alan Davies. His screams of agony were cutting into Massoud's head like a chainsaw. *Why couldn't he just shut the fuck up?*

Massoud had slapped the team's medic hard for letting the infidel get past him to stab the policeman in the belly. Then he had slapped him again for shooting at Smith as he ran away and missing. *The moron!* In a final fit of rage he bent down and slapped Davies across the face too, again and again until finally the man stopped screaming and lay there whimpering instead. He stood back up and looked down at the wounded man, lying on the ground and trying his best to hold his bloody entrails into his belly and stop them flopping out. His legs were smothered in a coat of blood and the iron taste of its smell was catching at the back of Massoud's throat.

"You stupid bastard!" he snarled at Davies. "If you were one of my men I'd put a bullet in your head!" Davies just lay there whimpering, pathetic in his fear and agony. Massoud turned to his medic. "You! Drag this piece of shit into the undergrowth; we're leaving him here." Then he turned to look at the man who had stepped on to the *Punji*

sticks. He was obviously in a lot of pain too, but was keeping his mouth shut, not daring to moan out loud and upset his commander. Massoud turned back to the medic who was dragging the whimpering Englishman away. "And when you've finished with him, give this soldier another shot of morphine, and make it a big one. We will go fast from now on, very fast! He needs to be able to keep up with us or I *will* put a bullet into his head and leave him here for the buzzards! Do you both understand?"
The two men nodded.

"Good! Get your act together! We need to move fast so that Smith and his bitch haven't got time to play any more stupid tricks on us. We need to drive them into the guns of our soldiers at the road junction."
He turned to the rest of the group.

"There will be no more rest from now on. We will push forward and *Allah* will help us push these infidels into the ambush that I have laid for them! Only then, when they are both dead, can we get out of this accursed forest and back to our sweethearts and families. Now move! Let's go!" Massoud shouldered his Mini-Uzi and set off at a blistering pace, his men falling in behind him with grim faces.

Alan Davies lay in the cold darkness, listening in absolute terror to the receding sounds of the Iranians moving away. He was in agony. The makeshift spear had dug deep into his guts, and, as Smith had mercilessly pulled it out he had felt his entrails bursting against his stomach wall, threatening to flop out. He had never been in so much pain and or so scared in his entire life. As the heavy silence of the Norwegian night closed in around him, he sobbed. He tried to raise himself by pushing hard on to a rock beside him, but he couldn't force his body to move; he was in just too much pain. His hand slipped back down to his guts, leaving a bloody hand print on the face of the rock beside him. He groaned at the injustice of it all and the searing pain, and thankfully passed into unconsciousness at last.

SIXTEEN

24th August
Telemark, southern Norway

As they hurried along the forest track in the brief darkness of the night, John Smith let his thoughts wander ahead. It was obvious from what he had seen the previous evening that their pursuers were not going to stop for the night and were marching forward in an effort to catch up with them.

But why now? That was the question that dominated his thoughts. In his head he envisioned a map of the area. He could see the track they were on, heading north towards a ridgeline and the main road, and beyond that a hard climb for a few more miles until they would reach the high-forested slopes of Brattefjell-Vindeggen. Smith hoped that they would be able to lose the Iranians in the vastness of this protected wilderness. But, for the first time since the pursuit had begun, he felt an uneasiness settle on to him. The Iranians were pushing hard behind him, almost as if they were hoping to herd him forward.

But to where and why? What could be ahead? He tried hard to put himself into the mind of the Iranian leader. Okay, it was obvious that Smith and Linda could keep ahead of them. They had already proved that in fairly tough country. *Were the Iranians hoping to catch up with them during the night or were they driving them forwards into something up ahead? What would I do if I was in their place?*

Then it came to him. *Of course!* he thought. *They're*

driving us forwards, doing their best to keep me and Linda moving because they've set up an ambush ahead!

He thought of the map again. *It must be what I originally thought. They must have put a patrol out on the main road ahead in case we went that way! That's what they've done. That patrol is going to set an ambush up and take us out as we try to cross the main road.*

Now where would I put an ambush? That's easy – they know we're going north along this track and they know that we will probably cross the main road where the track and the road meet, so that's where the ambush will be set!

Smith smiled in the darkness at Linda. She was doing very well indeed. In spite of the lack of sleep and the constant marching she was handling it well, and keeping up with the punishing pace that he had set. She was a marvel, this woman of his. He felt his heart swell with his love for her and with pride in how she was coping.

"Okay, Linda, let's take a breather for a few minutes. I can't hear them behind us so we can afford to rest for a little while." Smith reached over and helped her to slip off her heavy rucksack before removing his own. They moved to the edge of the track and gratefully sat down on a couple of flat-topped rocks. Smith leaned in close to Linda and gave her a one-armed hug, drawing her closer to him. He was surprised at the stiffness of her body as she pulled away from him. "Are you alright, love?" he asked.

"Of course I'm bloody well not alright! Jesus John, what the hell have you gotten us into?"

Smith was taken aback. Linda had shown no resentment at all during the previous hours on the march, and for a while he didn't know what to say in reply to her angry outburst. All at once he realised that he did not know what this situation must feel like to Linda. She was similar to him in many ways, and they surprisingly had a lot in common, considering their dissimilar backgrounds. But he knew that she wasn't a violent person. He respected the way that she always stood up for herself, but essentially they were totally different people with different feelings.

"I know it sounds pretty lame, Linda, but I'm really sorry that this has happened."

He felt her stiffness evaporate a little, but she was still angry with him.

"I know you are, John. The fact is though, it *is* happening. We're being chased through the wilderness by a bunch of religious nutcases who want to kill you, and because of you, they want to kill me as well!"

"You know that I won't let them do that, don't you?"

"Of course I do! That's not the point though is it? You're different to me. I'm a doctor and when I first started out as a doctor I took the Hippocratic Oath. I *swore* that I would do everything I could to help people get better, not to *hurt* them. Now I find myself sitting here scared to death and resentful of the fact that these people are after us, but you? It's almost as though you're enjoying all of this!"

"It's just that I'm good at this. It's what I do. I wish it could be some other way."

Linda put her hand in his and squeezed it.

"Look John, I've lived with you for a while now and I think I understand some parts of you. You're a very loving person inside, even though you can appear to be a cold heartless bastard on the outside."

They both chuckled at this, and Smith felt her thaw out a little.

"I really do love you, John. But is this what it's always going to be like if I stay with you? Are there always going to be gunmen popping up out of the woodwork whenever we settle down anywhere? Because if it is, then I'm not sure that I can live with it. I'm cold and hungry and I'm frightened. I don't want to lose you but I don't want to have to live like this either. Do you understand?"

"Of course I do. Christ, Linda, I don't want you to have to live like this either. But what else can I do? I didn't ask for these bastards to come after me!"

"I know, John, and I'm not entirely blaming you. If we

get out of this we'll have to talk and find a way around it, because I'm not prepared to live the rest of my life like this."

Even in the darkness he could see the flash of her smile and for the first time she returned his hug. Smith felt a great sadness settle on his heart. How he could he have put her in so much danger?

"I'm sorry that I've got you involved in this mess."

"I know, John."

"No, I mean it, love. This whole *fatwa* thing has got nothing to do with you and if I hadn't forced myself into your life you wouldn't be facing this danger now."

"And I mean it *too*, John. You *didn't* force your way into my life. I wanted us to be together as much as you did. I love you and these last few months with you have been the best of my life."

She hugged him fiercely.

"Then what do we do? I love you too but just by being with you I put you into danger. Even when this is over there will still be the *fatwa* hanging over my head."

"Isn't there any way that we can stop it?"

Smith laughed mirthlessly.

"Only if I go to Iran. The bloody Iranians are the only people who know that I'm still alive, apart from Davies and Helen Wright. I've already dealt with Davies, and I'm hoping that Wright won't be a problem, but if she is then I'll deal with her too. It's the Iranians that I'll have to sort out."

"But how?"

Smith's voice grew hard and he felt Linda shudder slightly against him.

"I don't know yet, Linda, but I promise you this - once we've beaten these bastards, I'll sort it out with the Iranians one way or the other."

As the brief darkness faded from the mountains and the pale morning sun rose above the horizon in the west, Inspector Lars Gundersen stamped his feet to try and bring some warmth back into his body and dispel the coldness of the night. He stood with a group of uniformed policemen next to the abandoned Land Rover on the track leading up into the forest. The group of men were involved in a desultory dialogue, not knowing what had happened here or what they were going to do now. They looked to the inspector for decisive leadership and action, not realising that at that moment Lars was as dumbfounded as the rest of them. The young police constable who had led him to this spot the previous night naively put the rest of the men's thoughts into words.

"What are we going to do now Inspector Gundersen?" he asked.

Lars scowled at him.

"It's obvious that something very strange is going on," the inspector mused, finding that the constable's words were at least getting him to put his thoughts together. "First we have the murder of the priest at the *Kyrkje* and the possibility that a dark-skinned man in a dark-coloured car committed the murder." He paused for a minute, his mind working overtime on the problem before him. "Then we have this very strange series of events here, not a mile and a half from the scene of the murder. It is obvious that whoever was driving this Land Rover was being chased by someone in the dark-coloured BMW below us. I don't believe in coincidence, so therefore the two events must be linked somehow, but how? That is the question."

There was a burst of static from one of the radios carried by the policemen and a brief conversation. The radioman presented himself before Lars.

"Inspector, Headquarters have come back to us with the names of the registered drivers of the two vehicles." He paused while he looked at his scribbled notes.

"This Land Rover is registered to a Doctor Linda Webb. She's an Australian national and her main residence is in Stavanger, but she is also down on our computers as having a second home in Flatdal, a farm house just at the bottom of this hill. The BMW is registered to the Iranian

Embassy in Oslo, Sir."

"Iranian? This mystery is just getting better and better," grumbled Gundersen.

He began to pace up and down as he mulled over the new information. After a few moments he clapped his hands together and spoke to his officers.

"Okay. This is what we are going to do. First of all get back on the radio to Headquarters. I want all of the information that they can get me on this Doctor Webb. Also, put in a request that the Stavanger police pay a visit to her home there and see if they can shed any light on this situation. Next I want you to get on to the Oslo force and request that one of their helicopters be despatched here as soon as possible."

He looked around at the men.

"I am authorising the unlocking of your weapons. It is obvious that whoever is involved here is armed and I don't want anyone from the service being put into danger without the chance to defend themselves. Don't worry, I will personally clear the use of weapons with my superior." He stopped the men from immediately rushing away to get their weapons with a raised hand. "I want you and you..." he carried on, pointing to two of the officers. "...to go down to Webb's farmhouse and see if you can find out anything there. When the chopper arrives, I will go airborne and the rest of you will carry on up this track to see if we can find the owners of these two vehicles. It shouldn't take more than an hour for the chopper to get here."

He searched out the radioman's eyes.

"Meanwhile, I also want you to get a message sent to the nearest Emergency Response Unit. Get them to bring their dogs. If the bloody Iranians are involved with this then we could be dealing with a potential terrorist operation. Right everybody, let's move!"

SEVENTEEN

24th August
Telemark, southern Norway

The sun had risen high in the sky by the time that Smith and Linda were close to the track's junction with the main road. They were both sweating in the midday heat and Smith could see that the forced pace of their marching was telling on his partner. Linda was almost exhausted and she sighed with relief as they stopped and stepped into the shade of the forest by the side of the track. He helped her to take off her rucksack and they sat for a moment getting their breath back.

They guessed that their pursuers couldn't be too far behind them but Smith was more worried about the ambushers who, he was sure, were waiting for them up ahead.

"Okay, Linda. Rest here for a bit. I need to go ahead and scout out the junction. I shouldn't be more than half an hour. I know you're tired, but keep an eye out for the bastards behind us. If you see or hear them, go further into the forest and hide yourself. I'll distract them away from you somehow."

Linda looked up at him as he stood and prepared to move. She wondered where he got his energy from. She knew that he must be feeling as knackered as she was but he showed no outward sign of his tiredness and seemed to be in complete control of himself, as always.

"Do you really think that they've got someone waiting

for us," she asked.

"Yep. Afraid so. That's what I'd do."

He smiled down at her and saw the worry lines on her face.

"Don't worry, love. If they are there, I'll deal with them."

He sounded supremely confident and Linda felt her fears fade away. In the short time that she had known him, John had never let her down. He was confident in his own ability because he had been tested, and had passed with flying colours many times in his life before. He was the toughest and yet the most gentle man that she had ever met. She knew that he had what it would take to get them both out of this horrible mess in one piece. She smiled back at him.

"Okay, I'll see you in a while, John. Don't worry, I'll take care."

Smith leaned down and kissed her on her forehead.

"I'll see you in a bit," he said.

Then he slunk away into the trees, making barely a sound as he passed out of her sight.

Ten minutes later Smith was crawling forward on his belly to the edge of the forest where it met the main road. He slowly and carefully pulled himself silently forward until he could see the road in front of him through a thin stand of tall grass. He had smeared some mud from the forest floor on to his face and hands and his green shirt blended well with the shadows and vegetation around him.

His position gave him an excellent view of the other side of the road and as he methodically searched with his eyes he thought to himself: *Now, where would I set up an ambush position? How about that clump of brambles? No, it's too thick and too far away. They're probably armed with the Mini-Uzi's, so they'll have to be within a hundred metres of the junction or their fire wouldn't be effective.* He craned his neck to look further and suddenly he saw it. The perfect spot for the ambushers lay about thirty metres from the junction. There was a clump of trees with ferns growing beneath them. He could see that the ground sloped away from the road just behind the trees, which would give his enemy the opportunity to lie down and be hidden from view. There was nowhere else that was as suitable. He relaxed, focused on the spot, and waited.

Sure enough, a few minutes later, he saw movement at the spot. The top of a fern trembled slightly and then jerked, as though someone had moved it from below. It was a windless day and Smith couldn't hear any birdlife about, so it had to have been moved by a man. He slowly crawled backwards until he was out of sight of the position. Then he silently moved away along the edge of the road for another fifty metres or so. Crawling forward to the roadside again, he could see that the road was curving slightly and that he wouldn't be seen from the ambush site.

He quickly scuttled across the road and into the forest on the other side.

EIGHTEEN

24th August
Telemark, southern Norway

Alan Davies slowly became conscious. He had passed out face down on the ground and as he tried to raise his head he felt pine needles falling from where they had stuck to his face, and heard them pattering on the soil. For a few seconds he felt quite peaceful and relaxed, but then the pain from his torn guts hit him like a sledgehammer, rippling through his body in waves of intense agony. He dropped his head to the ground and tried to clench his muscles to stop the horrid pain but it did no good. He just had to lie there and soak it up. Eventually it dulled a little and he opened his eyes to look around. All he could see were the bases of trees, soil and a few rocks. Mercifully the pain receded some more and he was able to push himself up a little, getting his elbows beneath his chest so that he could raise his head up. His eyes swam with tears and the inside of his head felt like it was stuffed with cotton wool, so it took him a few moments before he realised that something wasn't quite right about the picture that he could see. There seemed to be legs in front of him but he couldn't focus either his eyes or his mind properly. He tried to call out for help but his throat was dry and constricted and it came out as a quiet strangled garble. He strained to look up higher to see who the legs belonged to and gradually his eyes focused. When the sight before him actually sank into his brain, he cried out in terror and his head slammed down on to the ground as he passed out again.

The giant moose looked down curiously over his bulbous snout at the strange figure lying before him in the gloom of the forest. The man-smell emanating from it unsettled the moose, but he sensed that he had nothing to fear. He moved forward a few paces and lowered his snout until it touched the figure, then inhaled. The man reeked of blood and fear, and the overpowering acrid stench of it startled the huge animal so much that he skipped backwards a step or two. The moose raised his head, with its massive rack of antlers, and looked uneasily around the forest, suddenly aware of the closeness of death in this place. Gracefully he turned away and headed through the trees, eager to put some distance between himself and the thing on the ground, snorting his nostrils to clear them of the stench of impending death.

Massoud Hassan was beginning to feel the pace of the forced march. His men were doing well and keeping up with him, even the injured one, though he had a faraway happy look on his face from the morphine that he'd been given to relieve the pain. The unit's medic had approached Massoud at one of their infrequent resting stops and informed him that the man's wound was beginning to fester. If he didn't get proper medical attention soon, the medic had told him, he would be in danger of losing his foot. He might even be in danger of dying. Massoud had scowled at the medic and told him basically to fuck off. He wasn't interested in the injured man's fate, only in completing their mission as soon as possible and killing that bastard Smith and his bitch. Then they could all return to civilisation. The medic had acquiesced to his commander and backed off.

At sunrise Massoud shook out his unit into file formation, splitting his men so that they marched forward on either side of the wide forest track in two lines. He made sure that they were constantly on the alert in case

Smith tried another attack on them. He was pleased that his men were working so well. He would praise them when he saw the ambassador, once he returned with Smith's head in his rucksack as proof that he had carried out the *fatwa*. He smiled grimly to himself at the thought.

Inspector Lars Gundersen was also smiling to himself. He was beginning to understand more fully what was happening around him as new information flowed into him. The police in Stavanger had visited Doctor Linda Webb's house and confirmed that someone had recently broken in and ransacked the place. The farmhouse in Flatdal had not been touched, which fitted in nicely with his theory that the attackers had chased Webb into the mountains, perhaps surprising her as she was attempting to leave her summer home.

The Emergency Response Unit's Dog Team had tracked the woman and the men following her up the path leading into the forest and had just found a buried body near the top of the mountain.

Lars had spent the first few hours of the morning in the police helicopter, scouting forward of the dog unit, but they had found nothing so far. He had just left the chopper in the field below and had made his way up to the site of the buried body while the crew refuelled from a truck that had driven up from Oslo. Dr Telma Carlsen, the forensic pathologist assigned to the case, was already there at the site, and Lars smiled at her as he approached.

"Morning, Doctor! What have we got here then?" He peered past her at the body that a few of his men had dug up and removed from the shallow grave. She returned his smile.

"Good morning, Inspector. It's turning into a busy couple of days. This man is obviously from the Middle East." She turned, and bent forward with the policeman to look more closely at the body. "You can see that he has been killed by a massive blow to the head that has caved the skull in. There are small flakes of rock embedded in the flesh and if you look up at the scree slope you can see that there has been a recent landslide."

She indicated the mountainside behind them.

"Perhaps he was hit by a rock knocked loose during the landslide?"

She shrugged her shoulders to indicate that she probably wouldn't be able to prove the cause of death.

"Does he have any ID on him?" the inspector asked one of his colleagues.

"Afraid not, Inspector. We've been through his pockets and they're empty, Sir."

The police constable also shrugged his shoulders. Lars stood up again, stretching his back to relieve the ache that was there and rubbing his eyes through lack of sleep. He stifled a yawn, embarrassed that he was showing his tiredness.

"Well, it appears that a group of men, probably Iranians, are hunting our Australian lady doctor. But why they are hunting her is a question that I don't yet have an answer to. Interestingly, her close neighbours in the village report that she has been here since May and that she appears to be living with an, as yet unidentified man. Perhaps he is with her. Perhaps he may even have caused the landslide that killed this man."

"That would be hard to prove without an eyewitness corroboration," said the pathologist.

"Yes, that's very true. We must find the others that are involved before we get any real answers."

Lars smiled at the woman again.

"I'll have to get back to the helicopter again and continue the search."

He turned to the police constable again.

"Have you heard from the Dog Unit?"

"Not for a while, Sir. The last we heard they were making their way down into the valley on the other side of the mountain. Apparently they are following a good scent trail, but they're way behind whoever is out there, Sir."

"Yes. Let's hope we are not too far behind though!"

He clapped his hands together to help to restore the

circulation in his tired body. "Okay, I'm off to the chopper again. Please bag the body. I'm afraid that it will have to be carried back down to the valley. We'll never get a vehicle up here!"

"Yes, Sir. That's not a problem. Headquarters are sending out a team to carry out the recovery."

"Excellent! Right I'll be off then. Do you want to accompany me, Doctor, or are you staying here with our dead friend?"

"I'll walk down with you, Inspector. I'm afraid that there's nothing more I can do here."

NINETEEN

24th August
Telemark, southern Norway

Smith had worked his way along the opposite side of the main road until he was directly behind the assumed ambush position. His suspicion proved correct when he looked down and saw that two men were indeed lying prone behind the trees and ferns, one of them watching the junction with intense concentration. They were armed with Mini-Uzi's, as he had hoped, but they were in a perfect position to lay down a withering and effective hail of bullets on to anyone who was emerging from the forest track and attempting to cross the road in front of them. They were good at what they did, these men. Smith knew that he mustn't underestimate them. In spite of his worries that time was slipping by too quickly and that his pursuers would be catching up with them soon, he calmed himself and studied the men in front of him, thinking about how he would take them out.

The men wore the same type of clothes that the other Iranians were wearing. They were lying on top of some sort of groundsheet, and while one man looked forward at the junction, the other was obviously relaxing and resting his head on his extended arms. *They're probably taking it in turns to stay alert*, thought Smith. The men looked compact and fit, and if their pals were anything to go by, they probably knew how to handle themselves in a fight. Smith wasn't frightened of getting stuck in, but he wanted to be able to walk away at the end of it. He carefully studied the ground between the Iranians and himself and decided on a route that would get him behind them with the fewest obstacles that would make a noise. Carrying the Bowie knife with its fourteen inch long blade he began to slide forward.

Lars Gundersen sat in the co-pilot's seat of the blue and white Eurocopter EC135 helicopter of the Norwegian Police Service. He found that the twin-engine helicopter travelled surprisingly quickly for someone like him who was more used to ground pursuits. Lars found it difficult to see much below so he had ordered the pilot to slow down as much as possible and to get the chopper closer to the ground.

They covered the open area on the higher slopes of the valley and could see nothing of interest, so the chopper closed in on the forested lower slopes. It wasn't long until Lars became frustrated looking at tree tops beneath which he could not see the ground.

"This is no good. If they're in the forest we'll never spot them!" he said through the microphone on his headset to the pilot and the two observers seated behind him, looking down out of the side windows.
The pilot nodded in agreement and one of the observers said:

"There's a forest track running south to north marked on the map, Sir. I think it's just a couple of miles from our position. It might be worth taking a look. If there's anybody on it we'll be able to see them."

"If they don't hear us coming and take cover," replied the Inspector. "But you're right. It'll be better than looking for them in the forest."

"I'll keep us as low and as slow as I can, Inspector. That way the noise from the rotors will be much quieter than normal and we'll have a good chance of catching them unawares," added the pilot.

"OK. Go for it!"

Smith held the Bowie knife tight in his right hand. He inched his way forward over bare rock that was interspersed with clumps of tough grasses and ferns, trying to use the bits of rock that had a thick covering of moss to keep down the noise of his passage. He kept his body low in a traditional British Army monkey crawl, working forward on his hands and knees. He watched carefully where he lay his hands to make sure he didn't snap a twig or dislodge a piece of rock, then moved his knee forward to occupy the space where the hand had been as he moved his hand forward to the next place. All the time he kept as close a watch as possible on the two men in front of him, though sometimes they were hidden from view.

    At fifteen metres distance Smith lowered his body to the ground and took a breather, carefully wiping the sweat from his brow with the back of a hand. The Iranians still looked as though they were unaware of his approach and thankfully had not looked back even once in his direction. They obviously felt secure that no one could see them in their ambush position.

    Smith now moved forward using the leopard crawl. His body was down and touching the ground as he forced himself even more slowly forward using alternate knees and elbows, blade ready in case one of the men turned and saw him. He inched closer and closer to them, his eyes burning holes in their backs.

TWENTY

24th August
Telemark, southern Norway

To Lars, the Eurocopter also seemed to be moving forward inch by inch, though it was of course travelling a great deal faster than a man on the ground could go. Lars had had to make a choice when they came upon the forest track - to go north or south? He didn't have a clue which way the woman doctor and the Iranian men had gone, but to the south there was nothing but wilderness, while to the north lay the E134 main road. With a shrug of his shoulders he decided they should go north, that way was as good as any other.

Massoud Hassan heard the faint noise of the helicopter rotors when the chopper was still at least a quarter of a mile away. He was used to working with helicopters and calmly he gave the hand signals to his men that made them fade into the trees on either side of the track. The sheer speed of a flying helicopter as it rushed past and the drab clothing of his men in the darker shade of the forest edge would guarantee that they would not be seen by an observer in the chopper. The only thing that normally gave away soldiers' positions to passing aircraft was the pale oval of their faces as they looked up, but Massoud's men were all experienced and they knew to keep their faces pointing down at the ground and out of sight.

However, Massoud could not have guessed it, but

there was one weak spot in his well-drilled team - the man with the badly-injured foot. He was as high as a kite on morphine, and although he initially followed the rest of the team as they faded into cover, the sound of the thrashing rotor blades seemingly just above his head drove him to panic and lose control completely. He leapt from the trees into the centre of the path, where he stood with his legs spread apart against the downwash of the rotors. He looked up into the shocked faces of the Norwegian policemen sitting in the cockpit of the helicopter and opened fire on them with a long hammering burst from his Mini-Uzi.

Massoud, instantly realising what was happening and knowing that they were lost if they did not now bring down the helicopter, screamed at his other men to open fire, and the air was split by the thunder of five machine guns as they blasted dozens of rounds at the unarmoured and thin-skinned light helicopter just forty feet above them.

John Smith was just starting to position himself so he could throw himself forward on to the backs of the two Iranians when he froze to the spot. He had heard the not-so-far-off and very distinctive sound of a helicopter flying to the south of the road. He could tell from the stiffening of their bodies that the Iranians had heard the sound as well. He stayed put and waited.

The chopper appeared to be getting closer and closer and then suddenly the noise of the rotors was almost drowned out by the sound of gunfire cracking apart the stillness of the morning. The two Iranians jerked as though someone had just shot them, and half raised themselves to get a better view of the air above the forest to the south.

Let's do it, thought Smith. He launched himself silently forward, the blade of the Bowie knife glinting wickedly in the sun.

As the crazy Iranian man appeared from nowhere right beneath their noses and started blasting away at the helicopter, the Norwegian pilot acted on pure instinct. He jerked the collective to the right and rammed it forward as far as it would go. The two 452 kW (606 shp) Turbomeca Arrius 2B2 engines of the Eurocopter screamed almost with pain as they strained with the sudden massive input of increased power to push the helicopter up and to the right, away from the lethal spray of lead coming from the mad man's machine gun.

Lars Gundersen held on to the armrests of his seat for dear life and with terror-whitened knuckles as the pilot threw the chopper to the side and upwards. He felt the G-forces pushing him back into the seat almost at the same instant that the windscreen cracked and bullet holes appeared right in front of his face. He felt the hot breath as the bullets scorched past his cheeks and heard the grunt of pain as one of them found a living target in the back of the cockpit.

Then they were up and away from the danger, soaring above the top of the trees. Lars looked across at the face of the pilot and saw his own shock and terror mirrored in the man's face and eyes as he stared back. Suddenly both of them let out their breath in an almost hysterical laugh.

"Fucking hell!" shouted the pilot.

"I've been shot!" shouted one of the observers.

"But you're still alive, aren't you?" shouted Lars, looking over his shoulder at the man, who appeared to have been wounded in the arm and was clutching it tightly with his other hand.

"That was fucking close!" shouted the other observer. Lars grinned with the sheer exhilaration of still being alive.

John Smith set on his prey with the speed and deadliness of a striking cobra.

Neither of the two Iranian men, preoccupied as their thoughts were with the sound of unexpected gunfire in front of them, either saw or heard him move until the heavy blade of his Bowie knife thudded into the exposed neck of the man on the right. The wickedly sharpened blade sliced through the flesh of his neck and buried itself next to the man's spine. The Iranian's hands threw up automatically to protect himself but it was already too late. His carotid artery had been severed, and as Smith jerked the blade free of the clinging, sucking flesh, blood spurted out in a huge pulsating fountain. The man simply collapsed forward on to his knees, already dying.

The other Iranian was almost as fast as Smith though. He swung around when he heard the knife blade strike his comrade, assessed the danger in a micro-second and threw himself desperately backwards out of harm's way as he ripped his own knife from a scabbard on his belt. Smith followed and was on him in an instant, the Bowie striking out to stab the man in the throat as Smith threw himself forward, relying on his bodyweight and forward momentum to knock the Iranian off his feet and hard on to the rock beneath him. Smith grabbed the Iranian's knife hand, pushing the man's blade down and away from him as he leaned forward on his Bowie. It sank deep into the Iranian's throat, severing flesh and cartilage, veins and vocal cords. Smith lay there, all of his weight concentrated on his knife blade while the Iranian shuddered and jerked beneath him, his life-blood forming a large pool on the rocks. In just a few minutes, he too was dead.

TWENTY-ONE

24th August
Telemark, southern Norway

Massoud was fuming. Not only had the cretin with the injured foot, who was high on morphine, opened fire on the police helicopter and given away their position, but then even the combined firepower of his entire team had failed to bring the chopper down. He could see that it would take some quick action to pluck success from this farce of a mission.

As soon as the helicopter had disappeared over the trees he roared orders at his men. Within seconds they were formed up and ready to move on the track, even the fool with the injury.

Massoud gave them all a hard look.

"We must move and move quickly," he shouted at them. "Anyone who holds us up will die!"

With that he moved over to the injured man, looked him square in the face, then raised his Mini-Uzi and fired a burst into his chest. The man was knocked off his feet by the force of the rounds hitting him and was dead before he hit the ground. Massoud paused only long enough to spit on the man's corpse and yell at the remainder of his men to move.

They began to sprint up the track in a northward direction.

Inspector Lars Gundersen was also moving quickly. As soon

as the Eurocopter had escaped from the hail of bullets, he was on to the radio, organising his men and calling up reinforcements, his heart thumping in his chest from the sudden surge of adrenalin released into his veins from the brief burst of action. *I hope to God that this doesn't turn out to be another Utøya!* he thought as he ordered all Emergency Response Units in the county of Telemark to make their way to Flatdal as quickly as possible. The last thing he needed was for there to be a mass shoot-out like there had been at the island summer camp, where a lone terrorist: Anders Behring Breivik, had shot and killed sixty-nine young victims a few years before.

    Gundersen had at least twenty armed policemen at his disposal already, but they were spread out. Some were on the mountain following the Iranians and some were still at the village of Flatdal. The team on the mountain had made good progress and were almost at the junction of the path from the village and the forest track, led by the Dog Team. He ordered them to continue north along the track as fast as they could go. He then ordered the men still in the village to get into their vehicles and drive to the point where the track met the main E134 and to take up a blocking position there. Meanwhile he had another two Emergency Response Units on their way to the scene, one from Notodden about twenty miles to the east, and the other from Porsgrunn thirty miles south-east. It wouldn't be too long before they got here and he could position them to cut off any attempt at escape to the north by the Iranians, one unit supporting his team from the village and the other closing in to take the bastards down in a pincer movement with the team rushing up the track. Meanwhile he would fly east to drop off his wounded colleague at the village, and then use the chopper as an aerial command post circling high above the forest. All of his men were armed with Heckler and Koch MP5 sub-machine guns and P30 pistols and he was sure that they would have enough firepower to match the Iranians. He grinned at the thought of finally running these bastards to ground.

John Smith was also moving quickly. He dragged the corpses of his two would-be ambushers into the brush at the side of the road so that they were out of sight, and then he quickly searched through their pockets until he found the key fob for their BMW. He guessed it wouldn't be parked far away and pointing the remote up the road he pressed the unlock button. He was relieved when he heard the faint 'bleep bleep' of the car unlocking, although he couldn't actually see the car. He called quietly for Linda and they ran eastwards along the E134, looking for where the BMW was hidden.

Massoud and the three remaining men of his team pounded northwards, the breath rasping in their throats. None of the men dared to slow down though, even if the pace was beginning to tell on them. They knew that Colonel Hasan would think nothing of putting a bullet in them as he had with their comrade. They sprinted for their lives.

As they came to within a few hundred metres of the track junction with the road, Massoud let them slow down to give them a chance to get their breath back. His eyes darted forward, wary of another trap being sprung by that bastard John Smith.

TWENTY-TWO

24th August
Telemark, southern Norway

Smith and Linda found the Iranians' BMW parked just off the road about fifty metres east of the junction. When they reached it Linda stood with her hands on her knees, sucking in great lungfuls of air after their short but mad sprint. Even Smith was breathless.

Jesus! I'm getting too old for this shit! he thought to himself as he tried to slow down his own breathing and calm his thumping heart. *It's about time I fucking retired!* Despite these thoughts he looked at Linda's beautiful face, reddened by the exertion, and grinned at her, still feeling the adrenalin coursing through his veins.

"Let's do what one shepherd said to the other one," he said.

"What's that?"

"'Let's get the *flock* out of here!' This place will be crawling with cops before long."

"What if they stop us?" Linda asked.

"Don't worry, Linda. I won't kill any cops. I'll just hand myself over without a struggle. I don't want to put you into any more danger than I have already."

"Okay."
The relief was evident in her voice.

"Let's hit the road, Jack."

Massoud's team had slowed right down, weapons ready, as

they approached the last fifty metres to the junction. Even though they were all fit men, the last couple of days had taken their toll on them and they were all pretty much worn out. This had definitely not been the easy mission that they had all hoped for. That fucking bastard Smith and his bitch of a girlfriend had caused a lot of trouble and already brought about the death of two of their comrades. There was vengeance and murder in their hearts as they gripped their weapons even more tightly.

Massoud pricked up his ears when he heard the low growling of a powerful car engine approaching at speed. *It must be the ambush team! What the fuck are they doing? Where the hell is Smith?* he thought. He quickly got on to the radio.

"Amir? Rahim? Come in. Where are you? Have you got Smith?" There was no answer, just the hiss of static.

Suddenly the roar of the car's engine grew distinctly louder. The Iranians faded into the long grass at either side of the track, all except for Massoud. For some reason he knew in his heart what was happening. He expected the worst and just stood there.

A dark blue BMW shot past the junction on the main road. It only took a second or two but Massoud got a very clear impression of a man grinning at them from an open rear window, his hand outside the car giving them the internationally recognised two-finger sign for 'Fuck You'.

Massoud sank to the ground, the fight leaving his body. All he could think of was that one word that he feared above all others - *failure*.

As the sound of the car faded into the distance it was replaced by the growing wail of police sirens approaching fast. Massoud turned to his men emerging from their hiding places, their faces questioning and distraught. He felt a great emptiness settle on to his heart.

"Drop your weapons," he said to his men. "It's over. We've lost."

TWENTY-THREE

25th August
Telemark, southern Norway

The Norwegian forest was silent and still as the morning sun rose above the horizon and poured down her welcome rays of light and warmth.

Detective Chief Inspector Alan Davies of the Cambridgeshire Police Force lay where he had crawled to the day before. He had forced himself to move a few metres across the forest floor until he could lie back with his head resting on the exposed and gnarled root of a massive Norwegian spruce that towered above him. His hands still tightly clasped at the wound in his gut, and a congealed pool of blood lay around his midriff, soaking into the soil of the forest floor.

He had spent a nightmare-filled night, haunted by visions of grinning demons with coal-black eyes and missed opportunities, and had passed into and out of consciousness. He had lost so much blood that he lay there helpless, unable to move.

Davies could smell the earthiness of the forest. It filled his nostrils with its cloying stink and he hated it with all of his heart. *Fuck the forest and fuck nature*, he thought to himself when he was in his more lucid moments. *I hate the fucking natural world.* He raved in his mind. *Fucking Attenborough can have it! Give me the diesel and petrol fumes of bloody London or Cambridge or Peterborough or any other decent place full of teeming people. Anywhere is better than this God-forsaken fucking hole!*

But he raved only to himself. There was no one else within ten miles of where he lay. He could expect no succour as his life force slowly seeped through his fingers and soaked into the earth beneath him, no matter how hard he clutched at the edges of his wound, trying to hold them together.

Thankfully, the intense agony of yesterday had faded into a dull ache, though he swore that he could feel the pulsing of his blood through his veins as it emptied from his body. He tried to move, tried to force his head up from the tree root. But though he put his heart into it with all the willpower he could muster, he was so weak that he didn't budge an inch.

He tried to yell for help. Surely there must be somebody who would hear him? But his throat was swollen and tight and he could barely raise a hoarse whisper through his pale, bloodless lips. It dawned on him slowly that there was no one who could or would try to help him. No one except the Iranians knew that he was there, and they didn't care. They were the bastards that had dragged him into the forest and left him on his own. They had left him to his fate.

Tears flowed slowly down his face, drawing wet lines in the grime and trickling on to his lips, where he tried to lick their saltiness, thirsty beyond belief.

He passed in and out of consciousness as the morning slowly passed. When he was awake he pictured himself walking down a crowded street. He was the cock-of-the-rock, a king amongst lesser men because of his status and rank. He would look down upon the little people as they bustled past him: the van drivers and plumbers; the office workers and street cleaners; the bank tellers and school teachers. *Fucking civilians! Can't they see that I'm a DCI in the police force? I'm better than any of them and I can order them about and tell them what to do and where to go as much as I like. Fucking civilians! They're nothing!*

He sobbed with the injustice of it all. Here he was, one of the few, one of the elite, lying here alone in this fucking wilderness. He should be in the station fucking ordinary people about to his heart's content. Fucking up their lives, whether guilty or not, on a whim. He was better than the lot of them!

At one point he heard a sound in the forest behind him; soft padding steps through the pine needles. He suddenly remembered with fear in his heart the sight of the gigantic moose looking down on him. Or had it been a dream? He desperately tried to turn his head to see what it was that was making that eerie and stealthy sound, but he didn't have the strength. A smell wafted into his nostrils; it was powerful and musky. He lay there terrified.

Then he saw the fox. To anybody with any soul it would have looked a magnificent beast, with its gleaming red coat and long, bushy, white-tipped tail; a wild animal in the prime of its life. But to Davies it was just another scruffy, mangy bloody animal. *Fucking animals! I hate fucking animals!* he thought.

The fox looked at him thoughtfully. It could smell this thing's human scent and that raised fear in his mind. But the fox had lived its entire life out in the wilderness and had had very little to do with humans. It could also smell the overwhelming stink of blood. Fresh blood meant food to the fox, and he was hungry. He hadn't eaten for a day and a half. The smell of blood raised stronger feelings in the fox than the scent of humans. He crept forward on his haunches, cautiously, extending his neck to get his snout closer to that wonderful smell. He could taste it in the back of his throat, almost *feel* it filling his mouth with its wonderful taste. He got close enough to gently lap at the congealed blood from the human's wound.

Davies couldn't turn his head but he could still swivel his eyes to look at the wild animal that was licking at his blood. He tried to scream in his terror, but managed just a low garbled rasp.

The fox backed off at the sound that escaped from

the human's throat. But he didn't back off far. He lay there a few feet away, tasting the wonderful taste of the human thing's blood in his mouth. The fox was a hunter and a killer. He had the patience to wait for a while.

The fox just lay there and stared at Davies, licking his lips.

Davies felt himself rising out of his body. The awful agony of his wound vanished completely and left him feeling elated. He seemed to float above his own ravaged body, looking down on himself lying there helpless and alone. But he wasn't alone. He saw the fox creep forward again, body low to the ground and tensed for flight in case the human moved. The animal lapped at the congealed blood again, and when the man didn't move it plucked up its courage and raised itself up, standing over Davies' body. The smell of blood and food overwhelmed its senses and it pushed its neck forward, thrust its muzzle deep into the man's ragged wound and closed its powerful jaws and terrible shearing teeth onto a glistening piece of intestine.

Davies screamed.

Nobody heard him.

There was nobody there.

TWENTY-FOUR

10th September
Huntingdon, Cambridgeshire

Detective Sergeant Helen Wright sat at her desk in the Wildlife Crime Unit in Hinchingbrooke Police Headquarters. It was a small unit, with only a few personnel and very little in resources. Cambridgeshire Police did not believe that it was an important area in crime fighting, even though it had been proved beyond doubt that the illegal trade in wild animal parts in the UK was second only to the illegal trade in drugs, and like the latter was being run by organised criminal gangs, often by the *same* gangs. Many of Helen's colleagues thought that she was crazy for volunteering to take the position with the unit, but Helen knew exactly what she was doing. After all, she had a plan.

The telephone on Helen's desk rang loudly in the small, confined office of the unit. She answered:

"Hello. DS Wright, Wildlife Crime Unit."

The person on the other end of the line spoke English well, but with a heavy accent.

"Hello, Detective Sergeant Wright. This is *Politibetjent* Lars Gundersen of the National Criminal Investigation Service of the *Politi-og Lensmannsetaten*." He paused for a second. "Ah sorry, I am meaning to say that I am an Inspector with the Norwegian Police Service!"

Helen smiled to herself.

"Hello, Inspector Gundersen. How are you?"

"Oh, I am good. Thank you."

"What can I do for you, Inspector?"

There was another pause before he replied.

"Ah, I am calling because I have been told that you were a - what is the word I am looking for - a *comrade* of Detective Chief Inspector Alan Davies. Is this correct?"

"It's close enough, Inspector. Were you the one who found DCI Davies's body?"

"Yes, yes. That is correct. I am the one. I am very sorry to say."

"Well thank you for calling, Inspector, but I'm afraid to say that I was never very close to Alan."

"Ah sorry. Have you heard about the circumstances of his death?"

"A little, yes, Inspector. I heard that he was on holiday in Norway when he was injured while hiking in the mountains. I thought it quite strange as he never struck me as the outdoor type!"

"Ah sorry. The truth is that DCI Davies was murdered, DS Wright. Murdered in a very horrible way I am afraid. He was stabbed and then left for dead. His body showed signs of having been gnawed by wild animals and the pathologist believes it may have happened, how do you say? *Pre-mortem*?"

"*Before* he died? Oh that's horrible. The poor man!"

"Indeed. Horrible. I am sorry to give this news to you."

"Thank you, Inspector, for taking the trouble to call and tell me. That's very kind of you."

"Ah, not at all, not at all. To tell the truth I also wanted to 'pick' your brain. If I may?"

"Of course, Inspector! Anything that I can do to help."

"Chief Inspector Davies had been seen in the company of some other people that we arrested last month. They were Iranian people, but unfortunately they had diplomatic immunity and we had to release them into the care of the Iranian Embassy. They have now been expelled from our country. Do you know why he might have been with these men, Helen? Do you mind if I call you Helen?"

"Not at all, Inspector. I have no idea why the DCI might have been with Iranians. Perhaps he was working a case?"

"Please to call me Lars, Helen. No, I have checked with his superiors and they know nothing about a case involving Norge. Sorry, I mean Norway!"

"Well, I'm sorry, Lars, but I don't think I can help you."

The Norwegian policeman paused again.

"Ah well. It was a long shot but I hoped to have scored. Never mind! I am confused about his death and his being in Norway. But I am also confused about something else. The Iranian men appeared to be 'hunting' a woman by the name of Doctor Linda Webb. She is an Australian lady. Tell me, Helen. Do you know Doctor Webb?"

It was Helen's turn to pause, and to think quickly. She didn't want to be caught out in a lie, but then again she didn't want to implicate herself in Davies' mess either.

"The name does ring a bell, Lars. I know that I've heard it before but I can't remember where or when. I could look through my files on my computer for her if you like and call you back if I find anything?"

"Ah, no, it's not that important, Helen. Thanks. Doctor Webb turned up unharmed in Stavanger and does not know why the Iranian men were interested in her. Perhaps it is a case of mistaken identity? Apparently she was staying with a friend and did not even know that she was being hunted!"

"Oh, Okay. Well, I'm sorry that I couldn't help you any more, Lars."

"That is okay! There is one more strange thing with this case though."

"Oh, what's that?"

"We found some fingerprints at Doctor Webb's houses. According to Interpol, they belong to a man named 'John Smith'. He is the same man that killed those Islamic terrorists on the flight from the Gambia."

Helen couldn't help herself, she had to laugh out loud.

"I am sorry. This is funny to you, Helen?"

"I'm sorry, Lars. It's just that John Smith is dead. He was killed in an accident in a British prison!"

"Really? Then why have we got his fingerprints?"

"I expect it's because the records have been mixed up somehow, Lars. John Smith was also the criminal who blew up the Police National Computer in the UK a few years ago. Ever since then we have had many problems with our old records and mistakes are often turning up! I'm guessing that that's what happened here, Lars. John Smith is definitely dead. I'm afraid to say! The fingerprints must belong to someone else."

"Oh! Okay, thank you for that news, Helen."

He didn't sound that convinced but Helen didn't care.

"It looks like this case is so complex that we may never be able to solve it! I am sorry about your comrade's death though."

"Thank you, Lars. I appreciate you calling me, but as I said before, I never really knew the DCI."

"Of course, Helen. Well I will leave you in peace. Good to talk to you, Helen."

"And to you too, Lars. Goodbye."

"Goodbye, Helen. Goodbye."

TWENTY-FIVE

19th September
Huntingdon, Cambridgeshire

Helen Wright sighed deeply as she inserted her key into the door lock of her flat. It had been a long, hard day at work and she was exhausted. It was good to get home. She was looking forward to kicking off her shoes, sitting down in her favourite comfortable chair with a glass of wine in her hand and slobbing in front of the TV for what was left of the evening. She twisted the key, heard the lock turn and went inside. In the hall she took off her high heels with a deep feeling of relief and wiggled her toes about in the deep pile of the carpet. She sighed again with pleasure.

She went into the kitchen, selected a half-empty bottle of white wine, and poured herself a big glass, taking a sip to make sure it was still okay to drink. It was. She moved into the lounge, feeling in the dark for the light switch and flicking it on. Then she froze. Sitting in a chair across the other side of the room was a man. He was heavily bearded and his head was shaved, but she recognized him instantly. She'd been expecting to see him at some point.

It was John Smith.

"What the..." she started to say before gulping back her anger as fear suddenly flooded her system. She probably knew more about Smith's past than anyone alive and was aware how vicious and violent he could be if he was in the right mood. She hastily took another gulp of wine before speaking again. "John! What are you doing here?" she blurted out.

To her relief Smith smiled at her. He didn't look particularly angry or violent at the moment. However, Helen also knew that with John Smith appearances could be very deceptive. She felt the fear grabbing her heart and squeezing it hard.

"Hi, Helen. I'm sorry about scaring you. I didn't think it would be sensible for me to come and see you at the Police HQ in Hinchingbrooke. Last time I was there it was under very different circumstances, I seem to recall."

She saw the amusement light up his eyes.

It sure was! she thought. *You shot a senior officer from the Secret Intelligence Service dead, and the time before that you made a rocket attack on the building and totally destroyed the entire office suite of the Serious and Organised Crime Agency!*

"Come in and sit down, Helen. I'm not here to hurt you. Take it easy and relax."

Smith's black eyes bored into her and she almost felt as though he was reading her mind. She recovered a little and did as he asked, slumping down into her comfortable chair. Smith just sat there and looked at her for a while. Eventually she plucked up her courage and asked:

"So why are you here, John? You didn't answer my question."

Smith leaned forward and his eyes seemed to bore even deeper into her.

"I'm over here to tie up a few loose ends over the Norwegian business," he said, his voice taking on a hard edge.

"What I need to know is whether you are one of the loose ends, Helen. Are you a friend or do I need to deal with you too?"

Helen gulped.

"I probably saved your life, John!"

"Yep, that's very true. But *why*, Helen? Why did you help me?"

She gulped again.

Just how far can I push you, John? she thought. She suddenly decided to be honest with him. She didn't fancy the idea of being caught lying to Smith. She didn't think that he would take too kindly to that. "I'm thirty years old," she began a little nervously. "I'm a Detective Sergeant now, but by the time I reach forty, I want to be a Detective Chief Inspector, at the very least!"

"So? What has that to do with me, Helen? Do you want to catch me all on your own and prove yourself to your bosses? Is that it?"

His smile was feral now, like a wolf's.

"No. No!" Helen felt the first beginnings of anger creeping up on her. "I'm a *good* copper! I am *not* a wanker like that twat Davies! I need your help, that's all!"

"My help?" Smith sounded confused now. "What do you mean, you need my help? What can I do to help you, Helen?"

"You have contacts, and you have certain.....skills. I'd like you to help me with a few of the cases that I'm working on. If I do well and solve some big crimes then I'll get the promotion. That's all I want from you. Honest!"

Smith sat back and looked at her with a different light in his eyes. He sat quietly for a moment and thought it over.

"Okay. It's a deal. After all, I do owe you my life, *and* Linda's. I understand that you've also had my file removed from Interpol's records as well?"

This really surprised Helen.

"How did you know that?"

"Like you said - I've got contacts. I have a friend who does some consultancy work for Interpol. He told me. Thank you for doing that."

"That's okay! I've also had them removed from Europol's database and from the new PNC. What about the 'business' in Norway? Is that cleared up now? Is Linda okay?"

Smith seemed totally relaxed now and Helen felt her own body relaxing in response.

"Linda's fine, and thanks for that. She managed to convince the Norwegian police that she was innocent of any wrongdoing and that the Iranians must have got her mixed up with someone else. I lived in the bush for a week or two in Norway before coming over here. Once my loose ends are tied up we'll travel somewhere else and try and start again."

Despite herself Helen felt a stab of jealousy.

"So you will help me then?"

"Yeah. That's not a problem. It'll be a pleasure to work on the side of the law for a change, ha! You realise that I'm a mean bastard though, don't you. I won't do things the way that the police would do things. If I see a bad man I'll probably kill him."

Helen laughed.

"Good!" she said. "Some of the people that I deal with deserve it, believe me!"

"Talking of which, I'd like the name and address of Davies's Iranian contact over here. I presume that he had one?"

Helen smiled.

"Sure. Why do you want that?"

"He's one of the loose ends that I need to tie up." Smith stood up, ready to go. She thought that she knew what he meant by 'tying up loose ends' and for a moment she hesitated before answering.

"Okay. I'll give you his name and address. How will I get in contact with you when I need your help?"

"We'll swap info. You give me this Iranian's details and I'll give you my e-mail address. Deal?"

"Deal!"

They wrote their info down on to sheets of paper and handed them over to each other. Then, on an impulse, Smith leaned down and kissed Helen gently on the mouth.

"Thanks for saving my life, Helen," he said, and made his way to the door.

When he had gone, Helen stood there for a long time. She could still feel his kiss on her lips.

TWENTY-SIX

30th October
Kensington, London

It was the bedroom light clicking on that awoke the Iranian. He blinked his eyes, trying to shake off his sleepiness, and looked up from his huge comfortable bed to see the figure of a man staring down at him. His first reaction was to fling out his hand and feel for the panic button on his bedside table. The figure laughed at him.

"Don't bother, Mansoor. Your bodyguards won't hear the alarm. They've gone to Paradise and no doubt right about now they're laying into a couple of virgins each!" The man's laugh was sardonic and did nothing to quell the sudden rush of fear that stabbed at the Iranian's heart. He peered closely at the man but he didn't recognise the heavily-bearded face with its shaved head.

"Who are you?" he demanded, his voice sounding high-pitched and full of weakness even to himself.
"Wh.....what are you doing here? This is the property of the State of Iran. You have no right to be here!"
The stranger smiled, but it wasn't a welcoming smile, more like the smile of a cat when it's just about to dispatch a mouse.

"My name is John Smith, Mansoor. I want a little talk with you."
The Iranian felt the fear filling his throat at the man's name. He suddenly knew what was coming.

"I don't know who you are! You must have the wrong

person!"

"Don't be silly, Mansoor. Of course you know who I am. After all it was you that ordered your friends in Norway to hunt me down and kill me. I bet you they paid the price for failing though, eh? Where are they now, languishing away in prison somewhere in Iran?" His voice was still light and amused, but his eyes blazed with hatred and loathing. "Before you attempt to deny anything more, I have some news for you, Mansoor. While your wife and eight kids have been living in Iran...by the way, why do you fucker's always have so many kids? Haven't you ever heard of fucking condoms? Anyway, I digress, while you've been away from the little wife and kids and shagging the arse off your English mistress here in London, you'll be unhappy to hear that your little tart is in fact working as an agent for the British Secret Intelligence Service, and has no doubt been passing on all of your pillow talk to her bosses."

"I don't believe you!" was all that the Iranian could think to say, his mind swirling.

"No matter. I've been watching you for a month now, Mansoor, and I've followed your tart as well. She's been dropping off loads of info at a dead letter drop. I could have popped in to visit you while she was here, but that would really have put the cat amongst the pigeons, wouldn't it? I'd have had to kill her as well, and that wouldn't be very nice considering that she's only doing her job. Fucking you must be bad enough for her! But forgive me, I digress again, that's not why I'm here. I thought I'd just let you know about her betrayal of you for a bit of fun. After all, once you tell me everything that I want to know – that is everyone that you've passed on information to about me in your lovely country - you won't ever be talking to anyone else again anyway."

Smith's voice had grown more sinister and it dawned on the Iranian for the first time that this might be the end of his own life. He dug deep and found some bravery in his soul at last.

"You are a fool, Smith. I have been trained to resist

interrogation. I will never tell you anything!"
Smith laughed out loud at this assertion. The Iranian noticed for the first time that though Smith appeared to be unarmed, he was carrying a simple white plastic carrier bag in his left hand. Smith now lifted up the bag and with his other hand he began to pull something from it.

"You'll talk, Mansoor, don't worry. Me and my friends 'Black and Decker' here will make sure of that!"
The Iranian's bladder suddenly emptied itself with a gush, the stink of hot piss filling the room as he saw what it was that Smith was pulling from the bag.

It was a cordless electric drill. Smith laughed again as he flicked a switch and the loud *whirr* of the drill filled the room.

"Super, let's start with..." he began.
The Iranian screamed.

Author's note

I have written this short story in response to the growing army of John Smith fans who have asked to see him in print again, and quickly! I'm currently working on the next novel in the series which will be out in a few months, so hopefully this will keep you all happy until then.

I love John Smith. He's the sort of character that is a pleasure to write about. He's mean, moody and downright nasty, but he also has a good side, though he does his best to hide it from everyone. In addition he has a set of skills gleaned from his military training that are not so far from the truth for someone with his particular background. What action writer could wish for more!

This short story is also intended to set up John Smith in a new role for the rest of the series, as a man like him will never be able to retire completely. He will always want to right the wrongs that he sees in the world and he will also need to feel the thrill of being in action again.

I thought that the joining of DS Helen Wright and Smith in a 'fight against evil and injustice' would provide a good way of keeping the future books sharp and topical. Plus, I've got to admit, I quite like Helen's character as she's developed through the series so far and I didn't want her to disappear entirely off the scene. We'll be seeing a lot more of her in the future.

So, please see this short story as a prelude to the action and adventure that is to come in the series. I have some great new characters in mind for forthcoming books, many of them based upon real life friends of mine, and I will enjoy introducing them to you!

You can become a friend of and talk to John Smith (22 SAS) on Facebook.

Craig William Emms
March 2013

Also available by Craig William Emms: The first John Smith novels.

Printed in Great Britain
by Amazon.co.uk, Ltd.,
Marston Gate.